GW01099664

PUFFI

THE EXPLOITS OF

THE DIARY OF A

Satyajit Ray (1921–92) was one of the greatest filmmakers of his time, renowned for films like *Pather Panchali*, *Charulata*, *Aranyer Din Ratri* and *Ghare Baire*. He was awarded the Oscar for Lifetime Achievement by the Academy of Motion Picture Arts and Sciences in 1992, and in the same year, was also honoured with the Bharat Ratna.

Ray was also a writer of repute, and his short stories, novellas, poems and articles, written in Bengali, have been immensely popular ever since they first began to appear in the children's magazine *Sandesh* in 1961. Among his most famous creations are the master sleuth Feluda and the scientist Professor Shonku.

*

Gopa Majumdar has translated several works from Bengali to English, the most notable of these being Ashapurna Debi's *Subarnalata* and Bibhutibhushan Bandyopadhyay's *Aparajito*, for which she won the Sahitya Akademi Award in 2001. She has translated several volumes of Satyajit Ray's short stories and all of the Feluda stories for Penguin Books India.

Read the **Exploits of Professor Shonku** in Puffin

The Unicorn Expedition and Other Stories

Read the **Adventures of Feluda** in Puffin

A Killer in Kailash
The Bandits of Bombay
The Criminals of Kathmandu
The Curse of the Goddess
The Emperor's Ring
The Golden Fortress
The House of Death
The Incident on the Kalka Mail
The Mystery of the Elephant God
The Royal Bengal Mystery
The Secret of the Cemetery
Trouble in Gangtok

THE EXPLOITS OF PROFESSOR SHONKU

THE DIARY OF A SPACE TRAVELLER AND OTHER STORIES

Satyajit Ray

Translated from the Bengali by Satyajit Ray and Gopa Majumdar

Illustrations by Agantuk

PUFFIN BOOKS

PUFFIN BOOKS
Published by the Penguin Group
Penguin Books India Pvt. Ltd, 11 Community Centre, Panchsheel Park, New Delhi 110 017, India
Penguin Group (USA) Inc., 375 Hudson Street, New York, New York 10014, USA
Penguin Group (Canada), 90 Eglinton Avenue East, Suite 700, Toronto, Ontario, M4P 2Y3, Canada (a division of Pearson Penguin Canada Inc.)
Penguin Books Ltd, 80 Strand, London WC2R 0RL, England
Penguin Ireland, 25 St Stephen's Green, Dublin 2, Ireland (a division of Penguin Books Ltd)
Penguin Group (Australia), 250 Camberwell Road, Camberwell, Victoria 3124, Australia (a division of Pearson Australia Group Pty Ltd)
Penguin Group (NZ), 67 Apollo Drive, Rosedale, North Shore 0632, New Zealand (a division of Pearson New Zealand Ltd)
Penguin Group (South Africa) (Pty) Ltd, 24 Sturdee Avenue, Rosebank, Johannesburg 2196, South Africa

Penguin Books Ltd, Registered Offices: 80 Strand, London WC2R 0RL, England

First published in Puffin by Penguin Books India 2004

Copyright © The Estate of Satyajit Ray 2004
This translation copyright © Penguin Books India 2004

All rights reserved

10 9 8 7 6 5 4

This is a work of fiction. Names, characters, places and incidents are either the product of the author's imagination or are used fictitiously and any resemblance to any actual person, living or dead, events or locales is entirely coincidental.

Typeset in Garamond by Mantra Virtual Services, New Delhi
Printed at Anubha Printers, Noida

This book is sold subject to the condition that it shall not, by way of trade or otherwise, be lent, resold, hired out, or otherwise circulated without the publisher's prior written consent in any form of binding or cover other than that in which it is published and without a similar condition including this condition being imposed on the subsequent purchaser and without limiting the rights under copyright reserved above, no part of this publication may be reproduced, stored in or introduced into a retrieval system, or transmitted in any form or by any means (electronic, mechanical, photocopying, recording or otherwise), without the prior written permission of both the copyright owner and the above-mentioned publisher of this book.

Contents

Introduction

It all began with the fall of a meteorite and the crater it made. In its centre was a red notebook, sticking out of the ground—the first (or was it really the last?) of Professor Shonku's diaries. In due course, it fell into the hands of a publisher, and so everyone learned about the extraordinary journey that Shonku made into space in his home-made rocket ('The Diary of a Space Traveller', 1961).

When Satyajit Ray created this character for the young readers of his magazine, *Sandesh* (started by his grandfather in 1913 and revived by Satyajit in 1961), he could not have known that the first story would be followed by nearly forty others. In 1965, only four years after Shonku's maiden appearance, Ray introduced another character to his readers. It was Feluda, the detective, who created several new milestones in children's literature in Bengal. But even when Feluda rose to the top of popularity charts, it was a position he had to share with Professor Trilokeshwar Shonku. Nothing—and no one—could diminish Shonku's appeal.

The funny thing is, Satyajit Ray did not study science after he left school. Not officially, anyway. So what made him want to write science fiction? In answer to that question, he once said, 'An interest was always there. After all, my father (Sukumar) and grandfather (Upendrakishore) were both men of science, in addition to being writers and artists.' Satyajit grew up reading authors such as Jules Verne, H.G. Wells and Conan Doyle. It was Conan Doyle who inspired both Sukumar and Satyajit. The former wrote a parody of *The Lost World* called *Heshoram Hushiarer Diary*. In it, Professor Challenger became Heshoram, the intrepid traveller who discovered a strange land inhabited by equally strange creatures. Professor Shonku took his cue from Heshoram. Ray described Shonku as a 'mild-mannered Challenger'. Like Heshoram, he was initially supposed to be a comic character. Eventually, however, Shonku became serious business, although a steady stream of humour ran through every story.

In the early stories, Ray used the character of Avinash Babu to bring comic relief. He is Shonku's nearest neighbour and his severest critic. But, in the course of time, he becomes a close ally and serves a far more useful purpose. In this particular respect, he is very similar to Lalmohan Babu in the Feluda stories.

When these stories first began appearing in *Sandesh* more than forty years ago, not many Bengali writers were producing science fiction. Shonku's diaries opened the door to a whole new world, quite literally. They brought an awareness about things to which children had not been exposed. The word 'international' suddenly began making far more sense than it did before. Shonku travelled all over the world, met people with foreign names, mentioned details of foreign cultures, let fall snippets of information that the readers took in almost unconsciously, their 'learning' not once hampered by any obvious 'teaching'. Most important of all, these stories created a healthy curiosity about science and gave the readers a very good idea of what science could—or might—accomplish.

But all that was forty years ago. In the intervening years, Ray's detractors have not been silent. Some scientists have claimed to have found flaws in ideas put forward by Ray. As a matter of fact, I have seen a self-confessed 'authority' on Ray wave a dismissive hand and say, 'Oh, Ray was no scientist!'

Moreover, children today have not just read more science fiction, but have seen it develop as a special genre on the silver screen, both big and small. There has been *ET, Star Trek, Jurassic Park,* even *X-Files* and *Taken.*

What, then, are the chances of a simple old eccentric who lives quietly in small-town Giridih, with a cat called Newton and a servant called Prahlad? His adventures may be weird and wonderful, his inventions brilliant, but he offers no glamour, and no gimmicks. How wise is it to place the stories of Professor Shonku before a readership that is drastically different from the first lot?

This question was put to a handful of readers who have already read the existing translations. Yes, the stories are simple, they agreed. Yes, it may be possible to find one or two flaws, if one went looking for them. Yes, some of the early stories might now appear dated. But these drawbacks melt away before the sheer magic of Ray's lucid language, elegant style, succinct and graphic descriptions, gentle yet absurd humour and—above all—his ability to understand children, and show them, subtly and gently, the difference between good and evil, right and wrong.

Interestingly, the first English translations of Ray's works that appeared were stories of Professor Shonku. Those were done by Kathleen M O'Connell in 1983 (*Bravo! Professor Shonku*). Ray himself did some more in 1987 for a collection called *Stories*. In 1994, Penguin published another collection (*The Incredible Adventures of Professor Shonku*), done by Surabhi Banerjee.

Sadly, two of these three books are now out of print. But Penguin managed to retrieve Ray's own translations, one of which is included in this book. The other translations are all new.

The admirers of Shonku have waited for almost ten years to see this volume. I only hope that they will find their patience duly rewarded.

My thanks once again to Bijoya and Sandip Ray, and to Penguin India.

London
January 2004

Gopa Majumdar

The Diary of a Space Traveller

It was from Tarak Chatterjee that I got Professor Trilokeshwar Shonku's diary.

One afternoon, as I was sitting in my office, correcting the proof of an article scheduled for a Puja magazine, Tarak Babu turned up and dropped a red notebook on my desk. 'Read it,' he said, 'it's a goldmine.'

He had brought short stories for me earlier. They were not all that good, but Tarak Babu was once known to my father, and judging by the state of his clothes, he wasn't exactly well off. So I always gave him a little money when he brought me a story to read. This time, when he produced a diary instead of a story, I was naturally surprised.

Professor Shonku had disappeared about fifteen years ago. Some believed that something had gone terribly wrong while he was doing an experiment, and that had killed him. But others were wont to say that he was still alive. He was just hiding in some remote corner of the country to continue his work in secret. He would come out when the time was right. I had no idea if any of these speculations was correct, but I did know that Professor Shonku was a scientist. That he should have kept a diary seemed natural enough. The question was, how did Tarak Chatterjee get hold of it?

When I asked him, Tarak Babu smiled. Then he reached out, helped himself to a clove and cardamom from my little box of spices, and said, 'Do you remember that case in the Sunderbans?'

Oh God, was he going to tell me another story about a tiger? Tarak Babu had this most annoying habit of dragging a tiger into whatever anecdote he happened to relate. Irritated, I asked, 'Which case do you mean?'

'That meteorite. There is only one case, surely?'

Yes, that was true. I remembered reading about it. About a year ago, a meteorite had fallen in the Matharia district in the Sunderbans. It was pretty large, possibly twice the size of the one kept in the museum in Calcutta. When I saw its picture in a newspaper, it had looked vaguely like a dark human skull.

'What has that meteorite got to do with this notebook?' I asked.

'I am coming to that, don't get impatient. I went there in the hope of getting a few tiger skins. They are in great demand, and it's often possible to get a good price. You knew that, didn't you? So I thought, surely I'd find three or four tigers among all those animals that were killed? But no. Perhaps I got there too late. There was not a single tiger, or any other animal. Not even a dead deer.'

'Oh? So what did you do?'

'All I could find were some snake skins. And that notebook.'

Somewhat taken aback, I said, 'That notebook? You mean it was just lying there?'

'Yes, bang in the middle of the crater. When that meteorite fell, it created a massive crater. You've seen Lake Hedo in Calcutta, haven't you? Well, that crater was more than four times its size, I can tell you! That notebook was lying at its centre.'

'Really?'

'Yes. I could see something red poking out of the ground. So I went and pulled it out. Then I saw Professor Shonku's name on it, and promptly put it in my pocket.'

'A notebook . . . no, a diary . . . found in the crater left by a meteorite? Could it mean . . . ?'

'Read it, just read it. You'll learn everything. You write fiction, don't you? You make things up? So do I. This is far more gripping. I would not have parted with it, but right now my pocket's totally empty. So . . .'

As it happened, I did not have a lot of cash with me at that moment. Besides, I could not quite believe his story, so I gave him twenty rupees. But Tarak Babu seemed happy enough with that. He offered me his blessings and left.

Durga Puja started not long after that day. I became so busy that I totally forgot about the diary. I came upon it only recently, when I pulled a fat dictionary out of a bookshelf, and the diary slipped out from behind it.

I picked it up and opened it. At once, something struck me as odd. As far as I could remember, the colour of the ink had been green the first time when I'd looked at it. Now it was red. How could that be?

I put the diary in my pocket. Obviously, I had made a mistake. Maybe I'd seen something else written in green ink and confused it with the writing in the diary. Anyone could make a mistake like that.

My heart skipped a beat when I opened the diary at home. The ink was now blue. Then, an extraordinary thing happened. Before my very eyes, the ink turned from blue to yellow.

There could be no mistake this time. The colour of the ink was definitely changing.

The diary fell from my trembling hands. My dog—Bhulo—pounced upon it as soon as it hit the floor. It was Bhulo's major occupation in life to try his teeth on any object he could find. He did not spare the diary either. But amazingly, the teeth that had completely destroyed my new leather chappals only two days before, could do no damage to the notebook. Every page remained intact.

I tried pulling a page out, and realized that the paper was impossible to tear. It was like elastic—stretching if I pulled it, then shrinking back to its original size when I released it.

An odd impulse made me light a match and hold it against a page. It did not burn. Then I lit my stove and dropped the diary into the naked flames. I let it remain there for as long as five hours. Nothing happened. Only the colour of the ink continued to change.

That same night, I stayed up to finish reading the

diary. Now, I am simply going to repeat to you what I read. It is for you to judge whether it is true or false, possible or absolutely impossible.

*

Professor Shonku's Diary

1 January

A rather unpleasant incident happened quite early in the morning. When I returned from my usual morning walk by the river, I was considerably startled to find a weird-looking man in my bedroom. I screamed involuntarily, but realized at once that it was no intruder. I had simply caught my own reflection in a mirror. In the last few years my appearance has changed a lot. Normally, I have no use for a mirror, so I had hung a large calendar over it. Since that calendar was now old, Prahlad must have decided—without consulting me—to remove it this morning. I am tired of Prahlad's actions. He's been with me for twenty-seven years, yet it seems his brain does not function at all. Strange!

My scream had brought him running to my room. I decided he needed a little punishment. So I took out my Snuff-gun and tried it on him. The snuff in it is so potent that one shot, delivered somewhere in the region of a man's moustache, is quite enough. It is now eleven o'clock at night. Prahlad is still sneezing. If my calculations are correct, he will continue to sneeze for the next thirty-three hours.

2 January

My anxieties regarding the rocket are slowly ebbing away. The closer I am getting to my date of departure, the more enthusiastic am I feeling. I get more sure of myself with every passing day.

Now I am beginning to think that my first attempt failed only because of Prahlad. How was I to know that he had moved the arms of the clock when he was trying to wind it? In a complex venture like this, every second matters. Prahlad's mistake delayed me by nearly three and a half hours! No wonder that the rocket rose, and fell again with a loud thud.

My neighbour, Avinash Babu, is claiming Rs 500 as compensation. He says my rocket fell in his kitchen garden and destroyed the patch where he was growing radishes. That fellow is a bandit. His garden is all he can think about; he has no sympathy or concern for this huge project that was almost doomed.

I must try to think of a suitable weapon that can deal with people like him.

5 January

Prahlad is a fool, but it may well be useful to have him with me. I do not believe at all that it is only brainy and intelligent people who can go on an expedition like mine. Sometimes, slow and foolish people can show more courage than clever ones, as it takes them longer to work out the need, or reason, to feel scared.

There is no doubt that Prahlad is very brave. I remember one particular occasion very well. A gecko had fallen from the ceiling on my bottle of bicornic acid and overturned it. I was there, but could do nothing except watch helplessly as the acid slowly began to spread towards a little heap of paradoxite powder. All my limbs went numb at the mere thought of what might happen if the acid made contact with the powder.

Prahlad entered the room at this crucial moment, saw me staring at the acid, grinned and coolly wiped it off with a towel. Had he not done so, in just five seconds, my entire laboratory, that gecko, Prahlad, myself, and even Bidhushekhar would have been wiped clean.

So I think I will take Prahlad with me. Weight should not be a problem. Prahlad weighs 62 kg. My weight is 58 kg. My robot, Bidhushekhar is 90 kg, and all the other material weighs another 60 kg. My rocket can take anything up to 500 kg.

6 January

A few insects had got into the sleeves of my space-suit. I was in the process of shaking them out, when Avinash Babu turned up. 'I say,' he said, 'I hear you're off to Chandpur—or is it Mangalpur?—but what about the money you owe me?'

This was his idea of a joke. Any mention of science makes him burst into wisecracks. When I was building my rocket, he had said to me one day, 'Why don't you set it off on the day of Diwali? The local boys will find it quite entertaining!'

Sometimes I wonder if Avinash Babu is prepared to believe that the Earth is round, and that it rotates around the sun. Perhaps he would ridicule even *that* idea!

Anyway, today I ignored his jibes and tried to be warm and hospitable. I asked him to sit down, then told Prahlad to bring him a cup of tea. I knew that Avinash Babu did not take sugar in his tea, but a tiny pill of saccharine. I dropped a similar pill in his cup. That was my latest weapon. The idea came to me one day when I happened to read about the jeembhanastra in the Mahabharat. That weapon made its victim break into frequent yawns. Mine goes a step further. Not only does one yawn heavily, but eventually sinks into a deep slumber and is plagued by horrible nightmares.

Last night, I had diluted only a quarter of a pill in a glass of fruit juice and drunk it myself. This morning, I saw that the nightmares had been so terrifying that the left side of my beard had gone completely grey.

8 January

I have decided to take Newton with me. He has been walking in and out of my laboratory constantly over the last few days, and meaowing pathetically. Perhaps he knows that the time of my departure is now quite close.

Yesterday, I offered him a fish pill. He ate it happily enough. Today, I placed the head of a fish beside a pill. He chose the pill. So I need not worry about his food. All I have to do is make him a suit and a helmet as soon as possible.

10 January

Bidhushekhar has been making a strange noise every now and then, over the last couple of days. It sounds like a groan. I find it most surprising. Bidhushekhar is a robot, he isn't supposed to make unexpected noises.

The only sound one expects from him is that of clanging, as he moves about and simply does what he's told to do. I made him, so I know his limitations. He does not have the power to think independently. However, there *have* been times when he has shown me otherwise.

I can remember one occasion very well.

The idea of building a rocket had only just occurred to me. I knew that no ordinary metal or component could help build a rocket; it would have to be something special. So I began experimenting with various objects, and finally made a compound, using toadstools, snake-skins and empty shells of tortoise eggs. It was clear to me that what I now needed to add to it, was either tantrum boropaxinate or aqueous vellosilica, in order to get the perfect material.

'Let's try the tantrum,' I thought and was about to pour some out on a spoon, when a loud clanging noise began. Startled, I turned around and found that Bidhushekhar was shaking his head—made chiefly of iron—violently from side to side. That was the source of the noise.

What was the matter with him? I decided to take a look at him, and put the tantrum down. At once, he stopped shaking his head. I went over to him and inspected his insides. All appeared to be well. So I returned to my desk and picked up the tantrum again. Bidhushekhar began clanging immediately.

How perfectly strange! Was he really trying to stop me from using the tantrum?

I left it and picked up the vellosilica instead. Bidhushekhar clanged once more, but this time, his head went up and down, as if he was nodding in full agreement. Eventually, I made the compound with vellosilica and found complete success.

Much later, pure curiosity made me experiment with the tantrum. It would have been far better if I hadn't. I will never forget that blinding green light and the ear-splitting noise of the explosion that followed.

11 January

I dismantled Bidhushekhar today and examined all the machinery fitted inside him. Still I could not find any reason why he should be groaning from time to time. But then, such a thing is not altogether new. I have noticed before, that when I make an object using all my scientific skill, often it starts doing things I had not bargained for. Sometimes, it seems as if some unseen force is working with me, totally without my knowledge. But could that really be true? Perhaps I am unaware of the full extent of my own powers. I have heard that some really gifted and creative scientists have the same problem. They cannot gauge how far their own creations will go.

Another thought keeps coming back to me. It is more of a feeling, really. I feel an extraordinary attraction towards outer space. It is a feeling very difficult to describe in words. If you can imagine a force that is the opposite of the force of gravity, then you might get an idea of what I mean. I feel convinced that if I can somehow rise above the Earth, to a height from which gravity cannot pull me back, then this strange attraction will automatically guide me to a different planet.

It is not as if I have always felt such an attraction. It began after a particular incident, one that I cannot forget.

It happened twelve years ago, in the month of October. I was reclining in an easy chair in my garden after dinner, enjoying the cool October breeze. In the months of October and November, I spend three hours every night on my easy chair in the garden, for it is at this time of the year that a large number of shooting stars can be seen. Every hour, I can see nine or ten such stars. I really enjoy watching them.

That night, I have no idea how long I had been sitting outside, when suddenly I realized that one particular star appeared to be different from the others. It was getting larger, and it seemed to be coming down towards me. I stared at it fixedly. The star came right down, to the level of the trees in my garden. Then it moved to the west, and hung in mid-air—like a huge firefly—next to a flowering golancha tree. It was an extraordinary sight.

I tried rising to my feet in order to take a closer look, and woke up.

I would have dismissed the whole experience as a dream. But I cannot do so for two reasons. The first is, the attraction for outer space that I began to feel from the next day. It prompted me to think of building a rocket.

The other is that golancha tree. The normal flowers on that tree disappeared the next morning. They were replaced by a new, peculiar flower. I do not know if anyone has ever seen such flowers anywhere else on Earth. The petals of each flower are spread out like the fingers on a human hand. They look black in daylight, and hang limply down. But, at night, they glow as if they are made of phosphorous. And, if there is a breeze, they rise and sway. At that time, each hand seems to beckon me.

21 January

We left Earth seven days ago. This time, nothing went wrong with our timing, and we could leave on the dot of five.

The total weight of passengers and luggage that my rocket is carrying is 365 kg. Our food supply should last us five years. Newton does not have to be fed more than once a week. One fish pill is good enough for him to last seven days. For Prahlad and myself, I have taken the special pill I made from the juice of the fruit on our banyan tree. I call it Botica Indica. One tiny pill—the size of a homoeopathic globule—keeps hunger and thirst at bay for twenty-four hours. I have taken 200,000 pills with me.

Newton was restless during the first few days, possibly because he wasn't used to being kept in a confined space. Since yesterday, however, he has been sitting quietly on my desk, staring out of the window. The sky looks totally black, but there are endless bright, luminous stars and planets. Newton looks at these and swishes his tail at times. Perhaps those planets strike him as the eyes of countless other cats.

Bidhushekhar has nothing to do; he just sits quietly in a corner. It is impossible to tell from his round, expressionless eyes whether he has a mind, or can feel any emotion.

Prahlad appears to feel absolutely no interest in watching the scenery outside. He just sits and reads the Ramayan. Thank goodness I taught him to read.

25 January

I am teaching Bidhushekhar to speak. It is going to be a long haul, I can tell, but he seems to be making a real effort. Prahlad laughs at the way he pronounces each word, which annoys Bidhushekhar no end. I have seen him stamp his metallic feet in protest, and make that same groaning noise. Doesn't Prahlad realize how badly he may be hurt if Bidhushekhar struck him just once with his arms which are made of solid iron?

Today, in order to check his progress, I asked Bidhushekhar, 'How are you feeling?'

He did not reply at once. For a few seconds, he just rocked himself to and fro. Then he joined his hands and clapped, making quite a lot of clanging noises. Finally, he rose to his feet, stood straight, inclined his head slightly, and said, 'Goh! Goh!'

I have no doubt that what he was trying to say was, 'Good! Good!'

*

Today, the planet Mars is looking as big as a grapefruit. According to my calculations, we will get there in another month. The last few months passed without any problem. Prahlad finished the Ramayan, and is now reading the Mahabharat.

This morning, I was peering through my binoculars at the planet we are heading for, when suddenly I became aware of Bidhushekhar muttering something in a low voice. At first, I ignored him; but he kept making the same noise over and over. Clearly, he was trying to get some words out—quite a number of words, in fact.

I wrote them down quickly, as far as I could make them out. They made no sense at all. Then, as I was still trying to read what I'd written, Bidhushekhar repeated the same 'words', in the same tone. It dawned upon me then, that he was actually trying to sing! Or, at least, he was trying to utter the words of a song I had been humming a few days ago. I was amazed. Bidhushekhar's pronunciation of the words left much to be desired, it is true, but his memory was truly remarkable.

*

We can see nothing but Mars, when we look out of the window. The hazy lines on it are getting clearer. We should land there in about twenty-four hours. Now, when I think of Avinash Babu's jibes, I feel like laughing.

I have put to one side all that we shall have to take with us. My camera, binoculars, weapons, first-aid box—each of these things will have to be carried. There is no doubt in my mind that there is life on Mars, though I have no idea whether that life is large or small, peaceful or violent. Surely whatever creatures there are, won't look anything like man. If their appearance is weird, that may well scare us at first. But what must be remembered, is that just as we have never seen any of them before, they haven't seen any of us.

Prahlad isn't worried at all. He does not anticipate any trouble. I don't want to—

*

An extraordinary thing happened while I was writing

my diary a while ago. Bidhushekhar had been rather quiet for the last few days. I couldn't see why. He hasn't yet learnt to speak properly. He cannot answer questions. All he can do is try to repeat the words he hears.

Today, while I was busy writing, God knows what possessed him. He jumped to his feet, rushed to the control panel and yanked the handle that is supposed to put the rocket into reverse motion. Under its impact, all of us lost our balance and were soon rolling on the floor.

Then, somehow I managed to get up and press the button on Bidhushekhar's left shoulder. That incapacitated him instantly. He folded all his arms and legs and fell down, inert. I pulled the other handle on the panel that made us turn back and resume our journey to Mars.

What could be the reason behind Bidhushekhar's sudden fit of madness? I have decided to keep him switched off until we get to Mars. Then I'll switch him on again. Perhaps I had worked him too hard in trying to teach him to speak. May be that put too much pressure on his 'mind', so he lost it.

There are five hours to landing. The blue patches on the planet—that I had initially thought were water—appear to be something different. Besides, there are slim, red, thread-like structures. I cannot imagine what they are.

*

We landed on Mars two hours ago. I am writing my

diary sitting on a soft yellow 'rocky' mound. Everything here—the trees, the ground, stones and rocks—is kind of soft, and feels like rubber.

A little distance away, a red river is flowing by. It took me a while to realize that it was a river, as its 'water' looked like clear jelly, a bit like guava jelly. Perhaps all rivers here are red. It is these rivers that had appeared as red threads from space. What had struck me as water, it turned out, was grass and trees and plants. All of it is blue, instead of green. What *is* green is the sky. Everything is the opposite of what we see on Earth.

I haven't yet seen a living creature. Did I make a mistake in my assumptions? There is no noise at all, except the slight gurgling of the river. The atmosphere is decidedly eerie. Why is everything so quiet?

It doesn't feel cold. If anything, it is quite warm. But there is the occasional gust of wind that is very cold indeed. It lasts for only a few seconds, but seems to freeze the very marrow in my bones. Perhaps there is something in the nature of snowy mountains in the distance.

At first, I was afraid to taste the water in the river. Then, when I saw Newton drinking it, I felt bold enough to cup my hand and drink a mouthful of water myself. It tasted like ambrosia. Once, I had found the water from a fountain in the Garo Hills amazingly refreshing. But compared to the taste of the water from this river, that was nothing. One sip was enough to wipe out every sign of both physical and mental fatigue.

It is only Bidhushekhar who is still causing me concern. God knows what's wrong with him. I switched him on as soon as we landed, but he did not move.

'What's the matter? Don't you want to go out?' I asked him.

He shook his head.

'Why, what's wrong?'

This time, Bidhushekhar raised his arms over his head and uttered just one word. His voice sounded frightened. 'Denghah!' he said.

I have no problem in following his words. So I could guess instantly that what he meant to say was 'danger'.

'What danger? What are you afraid of?' I went on. Bidhushekhar's tone remained grave as he answered, 'Denghah. Teril denghah.'

Danger. Terrible danger.

He said nothing more, nor did he show any interest in joining us. So, in the end, we had to leave him in the rocket. Only Prahlad, Newton and I set foot on Martian soil.

*

It is more than two hours since we landed. The awe I felt at first is slowly leaving me. It had not occurred to me before, that a new place could have a distinctive smell of its own. I became aware of the smell here the minute we climbed out of the rocket. It is not coming from the trees, or the river or the soil. I have smelt each of these, they do not bear this smell. It is clearly something inherent in the atmosphere of Mars. Perhaps our Earth has its own smell too. We may not realize it, but if someone from a different planet ever went to Earth, they might sense it at once.

Prahlad is collecting pebbles by the river. I have asked him to tell me if he notices any living creature.

The green sky has started to turn red. It probably means that dawn is breaking. The sun should rise soon.

*

We have had the most terrifying experience on Mars. I have no idea how long it will take us to get over the shock completely. In fact, I am surprised that we managed to escape alive.

It happened on the very first day.

As soon as the sun rose, I left the mound where I was sitting and was toying with the idea of exploring further, this time in bright daylight, when a strong fishy smell hit my nostrils and I heard a strange sound. It sounded as if a large-sized cricket was chirping loudly: 'Tintiri! Tintiri! Tintiri!' I looked around, trying to figure out where the sound was coming from. But, at that precise moment, a terrible scream froze my blood.

Then I saw Prahlad. His eyes were bulging, his right arm was wrapped around Newton, and he was sprinting towards the rocket.

The creature that was chasing him was not human, nor an animal or a fish. Yet it had something in common with all three. It was about four feet high. It had legs and feet, but instead of arms there were huge fins, like fish. Its head was very big, in the centre of which was a single, large green eye. The mouth was gaping wide, but there were no teeth. Its whole body was covered by fish-scales, glistening in the sun.

The creature could not run very fast. It kept

stumbling, almost at every step. So perhaps it would not be able to catch up with Prahlad.

I picked up my most deadly weapon and ran after the creature, although I had no wish to use it, unless Prahlad got into real danger. It was not my aim to destroy life on this planet, without a good reason.

I was still about twenty yards away from the creature when Prahlad climbed into the rocket quite safely. What followed was totally unexpected. Bidhushekhar jumped out of the rocket and stood in the creature's way.

Perfectly taken aback by this development, I halted in my tracks. A sudden gust of wind rose at that moment, bringing with it the same strong stench. I wheeled around and saw that, from a distance, a large number of similar creatures—at least three hundred of them—were making their way towards us, swaying gently on their feet. They were all making that horrible chirping noise, 'Tintiri, tintiri, tintiri!'

Bidhushekhar swung his arm and brought it down on the creature he was facing. It gave a little squeak, flapped its fins and fell to the ground. Afraid that he might get carried away and try to tackle the entire Martian army on his own, I ran to Bidhushekhar and flung my arms round his waist. But that did nothing to deter him. He began moving towards the other creatures, dragging me with him. I managed to raise my hand and press the switch on his left shoulder. Bidhushekhar fell headlong, and stopped moving.

The Martian army was now within a hundred yards. Their smell was making me sick, the strange eerie noise they were making was almost deafening.

How was I supposed to lift and remove this robot

that weighed 90 kg? I called out to Prahlad, but got no reply.

An odd instinct told me to dismantle Bidhushekhar and separate him into two halves. I began loosening the screws fixed on his waist. I could sense that those creatures were getting closer. Out of the corner of my eye, I saw that there were now about a thousand of them. Their bodies shone so brightly in the sun that it was positively blinding.

Somehow, I managed to separate Bidhushekhar's torso from his legs, and dragged the top half back to the rocket, to leave it at its door. Then I began pulling at his legs.. The army was within fifty yards. My limbs had started to feel numb. I forgot all about my weapons.

When I arrived back at the open door of the rocket, still pulling and dragging Bidhushekhar's legs, I discovered that Prahlad had regained consciousness and had already lifted the top half of Bidhushekhar's body into the main cabin.

I hauled the rest up but, just as I was about to shut the door, I felt something cold and damp strike against my feet.

Everything went black immediately.

When I opened my eyes, the rocket was flying once more. My right foot was aching slightly, and a faint, fishy smell still lingered in the cabin.

How on earth did the rocket take off? Who started it? Prahlad knew absolutely nothing about the technicalities. And Bidhushekhar was still lying in two broken pieces. Did it take off on its own? If that was the case, where was it going? Where were we headed for? Which of the endless planets in the universe would see the end of our journey? Will our journey ever end, or are we destined to keep flying indefinitely, moving in an unspecified direction?

What about food? That will finish one day, surely. What is left will not last beyond four years. What are we going to eat then?

I have fiddled with the control panel and other machinery. Nothing appears to be working. Under such circumstances, the rocket should not be flying at all. But it is most definitely in motion. How, I have no idea.

A thousand questions are crowding my mind. I cannot find a single answer. From today, I have become totally ignorant, completely helpless.

The future is unknown, a deep, dark abyss.

*

We are still flying through space. There is nothing to see outside, so I've closed the shutters.

Prahlad has recovered to a great extent, and stopped giving frequent shudders. Newton had gone off his food, but seems to have regained his appetite. Perhaps it was a result of biting a Martian. I still cannot believe what happened. Prahlad's speech is even now somewhat incoherent, but from what he has told me, it appears that while he was collecting pebbles, he was assailed by a fishy smell. He raised his head and saw a funny creature that seemed a mixture of a fish, a human and some weird animal. It was standing nearby, on the river bank. And Newton was slowly making his way to it, his eyes wide, his tail erect. Before Prahlad could move, Newton leapt and pounced upon the creature, sinking his teeth into one of its knees. The creature gave a horrible screech and ran away. But, in the next instant, a similar creature appeared out of nowhere and started chasing Prahlad. What followed I saw with my own eyes.

Bidhushekhar, I must say, displayed remarkable courage. So I let him rest and take it easy until this morning, when Prahlad and I rejoined the broken pieces of his body. I pressed the switch on his left shoulder, and he spoke at once. 'Thank you!' he said clearly.

Since that moment, he has been speaking almost as clearly as any human being. But, for some reason, at times he can't seem to find the right words, and ends up sounding quite cryptic.

*

I cannot keep track of time any more. What is the date today? Which year is this? I have no idea. Our food supplies are sadly depleted, they will not last for more than a few days. I feel exhausted both mentally and physically; so do Prahlad and Newton. They are both lying listlessly in a corner. Only Bidhushekhar seems his usual self, totally unperturbed by any worry or anxiety. He is seen muttering to himself from time to time. I realized one day that he was simply repeating some lines from the Mahabharat that he had heard Prahlad read aloud, a very long time ago.

Earlier today, I was sitting in my seat, still feeling dazed, when Bidhushekhar suddenly stopped muttering and said more clearly, 'Wonderful! Wonderful!'

'What's the matter, Bidhushekhar? What's so

wonderful?' I asked.

'Wouldst thee open the window?' said Bidhushekhar. Although his speech is now quite clear, for some strange reason, he has taken to speaking old, theatrical language. We might be back in Shakespeare's time!

But now he wanted me to open the window. In the past I have paid rather heavily by not listening to him. So, this time, I stretched an arm and removed the shutter from a window. The sight that met my eyes was so perfectly dazzling, that for a time I thought I was going blind. When my vision became normal again, I could see that we were flying through an amazing, incredible area. For as far as my eyes could see, there was an endless stretch of bright bubbles in the sky—forming and bursting, forming and bursting. There they were one moment; and in the next, they were gone.

Countless golden spheres were expanding and enlarging, until they exploded and made a great golden spray of light, like a fountain, before fading away.

No wonder that I was totally taken aback by this sight. Even Prahlad could not help feeling enchanted. And Newton? He kept jumping up and scratching the glass on the window. If he could, he would have burst through the pane and leapt out.

*

I have not closed the window shutters since that day. It is impossible to say when the scene outside might change. I can think of nothing else, even hunger and thirst have been forgotten. At this moment, streaks of light are wriggling about in the sky, like snakes. At times, one of them might come very close to our rocket, lighting up the entire cabin. It is as if some king in this new spatial world is having a display of fireworks at some extraordinary royal festival.

*

What happened today, made us all break into a cold sweat—with the exception of Bidhushekhar, of course.

The sky was now full of huge, circular rocks. Each had craters, and we could see fiery tongues flick out of them. Our rocket was speeding through these rocks, slipping through narrow spaces to avoid a collision. Prahlad was chanting a prayer constantly. Newton was hiding under a table, trembling violently. Every now and then, it would seem as if we were about to collide with one of those rocks, but each time, as if by magic, our rocket turned away in the nick of time and found an escape route.

We were half dead with fear and anxiety, but Bidhushekhar stayed perfectly calm. He remained seated in his chair, rocking himself, and exclaiming, 'Tafa! Tafa!' from time to time.

This is a new word he has been uttering lately. I didn't have a clue what he meant by it, but earlier today, its meaning became clear. I was offering a fish pill to Newton, when Bidhushekhar suddenly shouted, 'Tafa!' and rushed to the window. I followed him and looked out. The sky was now empty. There were no lights and no rocks—nothing except a bright white planet, clear and pure like a full moon, looking down at us.

There was no doubt that our rocket was heading for it. If Bidhushekhar had to be believed, that planet was called 'Tafa'.

*

The scenery outside the window is truly beautiful. Tafa is clearly visible, and now we can see millions of blinking lights on its surface, as if they are myriad fireflies, glowing in the dark. Their light is strong enough to illuminate our cabin. It reminds me of the firefly I saw in my dream, back in my garden in Giridih. Each of us is happy today.

Perhaps our expedition will be successful, after all.

Tafa is getting closer every minute. Judging by its present distance, we will probably reach it tomorrow. There is no way of seeing any detail on its surface, except those fireflies.

Bidhushekhar has been talking a lot of rubbish again. What he has been saying is quite incredible. He has been extraordinarily cheerful these past few days, so I am beginning to think that perhaps his 'brain' is affected once more.

According to him, the inhabitants of Tafa are the first civilized race in the entire universe. Their civilization is older by several million years than that on our Earth. Every single inhabitant is a brilliant scientist. Since each of them is as clever as the other, they are finding it quite difficult to live with one another. It is for this reason that, over the last few years, they have been 'importing' less intelligent people from other planets and getting them to live in Tafa.

'Is that so?' I asked, 'In that case, they should find it quite useful to have Prahlad around, wouldn't you say?' At this remark, Bidhushekhar broke into a guffaw and began clapping. He made such an awful racket that I was obliged to press the switch on his shoulder.

*

We reached Tafa yesterday. When I climbed out of the rocket, I saw that a large number of people had gathered to welcome me. I am referring to them as 'people', but they don't look like normal people at all. If one can imagine what a giant ant might look like, one will get an idea of their appearance. Their heads are large, and so are their eyes, but their arms and legs are very thin, as if they have no use for their limbs.

There is no doubt that what Bidhushekhar had told me about them is wholly untrue. In fact, I think the truth is just the opposite. That is to say, these creatures are far behind our human civilization. It will take them thousands of years to catch up with the human race.

The way they live is totally primitive, compared to our own lifestyle. There are no buildings or houses in Tafa, nor are there trees and plants. The inhabitants appear to live underground; they just disappear into holes. But they have given me a proper house to live in. It is exactly like my house in Giridih, except that it does not have a laboratory.

Prahlad and Newton are fine. They have settled down very well, and do not seem to be even aware that they are on a different planet, living in a totally different atmosphere.

Only Bidhushekhar has disappeared. He vanished almost as soon as we got here. Perhaps, having told me a pack of lies about these people, he is too embarrassed to face me.

I have decided to stop writing my diary after today, as I do not see any chance of anything happening here that might be worth recording. My only regret is that there is no way of sending my diary back to Earth. It is packed with such a lot of valuable information. The fools who live here will never understand its meaning, nor will they let me go back.

To tell the truth, I am in no hurry to go back to Earth, for I am being very well looked after here. Perhaps these creatures think they can get a lot out of me.

How they learnt to speak in any language, I do not know. But the advantage in being able to communicate is that if I scold any of them, the creature can understand my words. Only the other day, I called an ant and said, 'Well, where are your scientists and all those clever people I have heard about? Let me speak to them. You lot are running so far behind us humans!'

The ant replied, 'What will you do with scientists, or science? Why don't you just stay the way you are? We'll visit you from time to time, all right? We find your plain and simple words, your naivete most entertaining!'

What impertinence!

Highly incensed, I took my Snuff-gun and fired it directly at the ant's nostrils. But nothing happened. The ant remained quite unaffected.

The reason was clear. These creatures haven't even learnt to sneeze!

*

[Readers might wonder where I have kept Professor Shonku's diary, and whether one might see this remarkable object. What I wanted to do was to have the paper and ink examined by a scientist, and then I would have handed it over to a museum. Anyone could have gone and looked at it there. But there is no way of doing that now.

The day I finished making a copy of the entire diary and dropped it off at the press for printing, an amazing thing happened. I returned home and went to my bedroom to get the original diary from the bookshelf. The space it had been occupying was empty. All that remained of the diary was a small piece of its red cover, and a few pages, chewed to a powder. Nearly a hundred hungry black ants were still crawling all over these remnants. They had eaten the entire diary. What little remained, vanished before my eyes. All I could do was stare in disbelief.

The object that had appeared completely indestructible, finally turned into fodder for black ants. For the life of me, I cannot see how that could happen.

Can you think of a reason?]

Translated by Gopa Majumdar

PROFESSOR SHONKU AND THE BONES

[The famous scientist, Professor Shonku, has been missing for several years. We came upon one of his diaries purely by chance, and published it in *Sandesh* ('The Diary of a Space Traveller'). Then I made a number of enquiries and finally managed to visit his house in Giridih, where I was able to go through his papers and other research material kept in his laboratory. Among those were twenty-one diaries. I have read some of them already, and am now reading the rest. Each of them records an amazing and extraordinary experience. What follows is one such account. I hope to let you read more of his diaries in the future.]

7 May

I am writing my diary by the light of a petromax, sitting

in a cave in the foothills of the Nilgiris. The terrain outside the cave is uneven; a large area is dotted with rocky mounds. There aren't many trees, except a large peepal just outside the cave.

Close to where I am sitting, filling nearly half the cave, are heaps of bones—the result of my tireless research and sheer hard work over the last seventeen days. I have read a lot about prehistoric animals. Judging by all that I have learnt, this animal is wholly unknown to man. Its size is colossal. Its one foot measures three-and-a-half feet. Its ribs are so large that I think two adult humans could easily live within its rib-cage. Its forelegs, however, are comparatively smaller—a bit like those of a tyrannosaurus. There is a tail which is quite long and thick. But what is most interesting, is that there are hints of two tiny wings, although there would be no question of such a massive creature flying with the help of those.

Collecting these bones and removing them into this cave was a very difficult task. The local adivasis helped a lot. If they hadn't, I could not have achieved much with only Prahlad to help me. I had no wish to publicize my venture and make a great song and dance about a new archaeological mission. I have always preferred working quietly on my own. Besides, there was a degree of uncertainty in this particular venture. I did have an idea that there might be the bones of a prehistoric animal on this side of the Nilgiris, but of course I could not be sure. In this line of work no one can ever be totally certain of the outcome. Even large and well-organized archaeological projects are sometimes doomed to failure.

Perhaps I should explain here why I became so interested in bones. I am a scientist; my work is usually related to physics. So why am I suddenly so passionate about archaeology?

The answer to this question lies in something that happened three years ago. That particular incident occupies a special place in my memory, though I have had many a strange and weird experience.

It happened in the summer, in May. I was sitting in my living room one evening, having a cup of coffee, when Avinash Babu turned up. Usually, he makes some snide remark or another about my experiments, and I find that most irritating. But on that particular day, I had a trick up my sleeve that I knew would silence him.

Without saying a word, I offered him a new fruit from my tree.

Avinash Babu took it, turned it over, looked at it carefully, and said, 'I say, I've never seen anything like this! It smells like mango, but doesn't look like it. And it's round, like an orange, but so totally smooth!'

'Let me get you a knife. You can cut yourself a piece,' I told him.

A couple of minutes later, Avinash Babu put a piece of the fruit in his mouth and went into raptures. 'Aaah! This is absolutely wonderful! Is this fruit grown in this country, or has it come from abroad? Where did you get it? What's it called?'

I took him out into the garden and showed him the tree that had borne that fruit. I called it mangorange, for it was a mixture of mango and orange. It had taken me a whole year to develop that tree. 'Next time,' I said,

'I am going to mix more than two kinds of fruit. There are endless possibilities of creating new and extraordinary fruit—be it in taste, smell or nourishment.'

When we returned to the living room, Avinash Babu flopped down on a sofa and exclaimed, 'Hey! I haven't yet told you why I came here, have I? All this business of your new fruit distracted me. It's about a sadhu. Do you know the silk-cotton tree just beyond the cremation ground? That's where he lives.'

'What do you mean? He's living *in* the tree?'

'Yes, he practises yoga from the tree. He places his feet round a branch, and hangs upside down. His arms hang down, too. He does it every day, he's perfectly used to it.'

'Humbug! It's just a trick.'

It is not that I have no respect for sadhus, but there is a limit to how far that respect will go. My past experience has shown me, more than once, that most of them are frauds.

Avinash Babu, however, became quite agitated at my words. He thumped the table so hard that it nearly knocked my coffee cup over. Then he said, 'No, sir. This man is no fraud. He knows sanjeevani mantra . . . you know, the art of reviving the dead.'

'How does he do it?'

'Very simply. If anyone brings him the bones of a dead animal, he chants a prayer and those bones are covered by flesh and blood and skin, and then you have a live animal again. The first day, he revived a dead jackal. My servant, Banchharam, saw it happen with his own eyes, and came and told me. At first, like you, I didn't believe the story. So I told him not to be silly. But, later in the afternoon, I felt so curious about this sadhu baba that I wanted to go and look at him myself. Do you know what I saw? Well, Noni Ghosh had a calf. A month ago, it had strayed towards the railway tracks. That's where it died, possibly bitten by a snake. Vultures finished it off, all except its bones. A shepherd boy saw those bones and brought them over to the sadhu. When I got there, the sadhu was still hanging upside down, but looking straight at the heap of bones.

'He was rolling his eyes and swinging his arms. Then, suddenly, he raised his left arm and pointed it west. His right arm remained hanging down, but now he was rotating it very fast. And he was muttering something. You will not believe it, I know, but the next thing I saw was those bones disappear under layers of flesh; then that was covered by skin and hair and hooves and everything. The calf opened its eyes, and sprang to its feet—as if it had simply been sleeping—and ran away, mooing loudly. I have heard of mass hypnotism—I believe some great magicians can hypnotise a large number of people. But, in this case, even that doesn't apply, does it? I just saw that calf again, on my way here, moving about quite normally. So I thought it might be fun to take you along to see that sadhu, since you are such a great sceptic. Will you come with me to the cremation ground?'

I thought it over. If I didn't go with Avinash Babu, there was no way of making sure that he was telling the truth. The whole thing might well mean a complete waste of time, but it should not take more than an hour. So, in the end, I agreed.

By the time we reached the river Usri, passed the cremation ground and found the silk-cotton tree, only fifteen minutes were left before sunset.

The sadhu's appearance took me by surprise. I had not expected him to look the way he did. He was very dark, his height was in the region of six feet, his hair and beard totally black and very thick. It was impossible to guess his age. If an ordinary man tried to hang upside down from a tree, in the same manner as the sadhu, after a point all his blood would rush to his head and he would most certainly die. But this man was showing no sign of discomfort. On the contrary, it seemed to me as if there was a hint of a smile on his lips.

About fifty people had gathered round the tree. Perhaps another 'magic' session was about to begin.

Avinash Babu pushed his way through the crowd, dragging me with him. Now I could see more clearly. Just under the sadhu's head was a pile of bones, belonging perhaps to a cat, or some animal of that size. The sadhu's palms were joined, and all his fingers were pointed at the bones. Suddenly, he gave a loud roar, and began swinging from the tree. His eyes remained fixed on the bones. Avinash Babu clutched my sleeve.

Perhaps I should mention here that I have done a great deal of research in hypnotism, and can say, with some confidence, that no magician on earth can hypnotize me. Many world-famous magicians—such as Wily, Maxim-the-Great, Fabulino, John Shamrock—have tried and failed. Once, a Russian magician called Zebulski tried so hard that he fainted himself! Anyway, the point is that, if that sadhu was going to use hypnotism as a weapon, I was bound to catch him out.

After about a minute, he stopped swinging and became still. I noticed that his whole body was trembling, but the tremble was so faint that I don't think anyone else noticed it.

Then I looked at the bones, and spotted another amazing factor. They were moving. Gently and faintly, but there could be no mistake. They were rattling against one another, making a slight clicking noise, the kind of noise chattering teeth make when it is very cold.

'Doesn't he chant a mantra or something?' I whispered into Avinash Babu's ear.

'Sh-sh, wait. Your patience will be duly rewarded,' he whispered back, laying a finger on his lips.

I did not have to wait long. A jackal cried out from the woods on the other side of the river and, at that precise moment, the sadhu raised his left arm and pointed it at the setting sun. Then he began rotating his right arm, as fast as an electric fan. This was followed by a strange noise that seemed to come out of his mouth. If this was the famous sanjeevani mantra, then obviously it had to remain a complete mystery to ordinary, normal men. It sounded as if the speed on a gramophone had been raised to an extraordinary pitch. The voice was thin and squeaky, the words came very quickly. I could not have imagined that a man could possibly speak in a voice like that, and utter words at that speed.

My eyes went back to the bones.

I am a scientist. I do not know if the things that I saw next, could have any scientific basis. May be they could; may be they did. Perhaps, in fifty years, science will be able to explain it; but certainly at this moment, all of it is incredible. Yet, I cannot deny what I saw very clearly, with my own eyes.

What was just a heap of loose bones, soon disappeared. Each bone clicked into place—that is to say, the ribs joined to form a rib-cage, the skull settled on top of the body, the bones meant for the legs went to the right place. In a matter of seconds appeared flesh, veins, blood, nerves, hair, nails, eyes and, finally, life. As soon as life was restored, the erstwhile heap of bones turned into a bright white rabbit. Its red eyes darted here and there for a few moments; then it flicked its long ears a couple of times, before leaping up and hopping away, making its way through people's legs.

I returned home profoundly startled and lost in thought. For the first time, I had no answer for Avinash Babu. I was stumped. He walked me back to my house and said, somewhat sarcastically, 'You only know what you've read in books. For twenty years, my dear sir, you have handled acids, and God knows what else, in your lab. All you managed to show for it was burnt and injured hands. Now, please stop this nonsense and come and join me in my farm. We could grow potatoes together!'

The next day, I realized that I could no longer concentrate on my work. My mind kept going back to that silk-cotton tree. Two days later, I could not contain myself any more. I went back to watch the sadhu at work. And I went again the following day. On the first day, he revived a dead dog, and on the second day, a parrot. The dog was said to have gone mad before it died. When its skeleton was brought back to life, the first thing it did was bite our Moti dhobi's leg. The parrot flew straight up to the tree, perched on its top branch and began chanting, 'Radha-Krishna! Radha-Krishna!'

I returned home with a heavy heart.

Try as I might, I just could not make any sense out of that mantra. Yet, if I could somehow understand its meaning, it might go a long way in solving this mystery.

The next evening, an idea suddenly came into my head. It was so brilliant that I had to applaud myself.

I had a tape recorder. Couldn't I tape that mantra secretly? Of course I could, and I must do it as soon as possible. Who knew when the sadhu might disappear?

The following night was a moonless one. The microphone of my recorder was no larger than a matchbox. I attached a long wire to it, and went to the cremation ground in the middle of the night.

As I approached the silk-cotton tree, I could see around thirty people still gathered under the sadhu. His fame had clearly spread far and wide. The presence of so many people was most helpful. I could lose myself in the crowd, then pretend to go round the trunk of the tree, as if paying my respects to the holy man. In so doing, I could quickly slip the microphone into a hollow in the tree. Then I moved away, and hid the other end of the wire behind a flowering shrub, about twenty yards away.

The next day, one of the locals called Hanuman Misra brought his dead goat's bones to the sadhu. While it was being restored to life, that strange mantra was recorded on my machine.

By the time I collected the recorder and returned home late in the evening, walking stealthily like a thief, it had started to rain. I asked Prahlad to make me a hot cup of coffee, and went straight to my laboratory.

Lightning flashed a couple of times, and there was a clap of thunder. The rain became heavier. I closed all the windows, placed the recorder on a table, and plugged the wire into a socket in the wall. What I wanted to do, was listen to the mantra first at normal speed; then I would reduce the speed by half. The words were bound to become clear if they were spoken more slowly. If that happened, that sadhu with magical powers—who could conquer death—would be defeated at the hands of science.

I sipped the coffee Prahlad had just brought in and pressed a switch. The brown magnetic tape began whirring instantly.

'*Bolo hori, horibol!*'

It was a different and familiar chant, uttered by people who had carried a corpse to the cremation ground a few minutes before the sadhu began his show. My recorder had picked it up.

A jackal cried out from the machine. Then a takshak snake. Right, it was now time for the mantra to begin.

There it was—that same thin, sharp voice, those same words muttered incredibly quickly . . . exactly as I'd heard before . . . but what was this? Why did my machine suddenly come to a stop?

And who was laughing in my room? So uproariously, filling the room with a loud, raucous guffaw? It was not something the recorder had picked up. It was there . . . just outside my room . . . !

My eyes fell on the eastern window. Outside it was my garden and, in that garden, the golancha tree.

Lightning flashed once more. In that instant, I saw that sadhu hanging upside down from a branch of the golancha tree. His eyes, filled with an angry, vindictive look, were fixed on my recorder.

The whole thing struck me as so totally incredible that I felt no fear, no anxiety. I got up and pushed the window open.

But where was the sadhu? He was gone. The tree was there, its leaves glistening in the rain. Of the sadhu there was no sign. He had vanished.

Had I made a mistake? Was I seeing things? How could both my eyes and ears deceive me? Didn't I just hear his laughter? His voice had become quite familiar to me in the last three days.

Anyway, whether he had really been in my garden, or whether it was an act of magic, now he was most definitely gone. I saw no point in worrying about him any more, and decided to play my machine once again.

To my surprise, when I pressed its switch, it began working at once. But where were the sounds I had recorded earlier? How did that awful laughter get recorded instead of the mantra? The mantra was wiped clean.

I felt crushed once more. That sadhu, I had to admit, did have some supernatural powers. He had realized what I had done, and had arrived here to destroy my secret plans.

Now there was no way of learning the sanjeevani mantra.

*

The next day, Avinash Babu paid me another visit. 'The sadhu has left,' he told me. 'That tree is now empty, there's no one hanging from it. In fact, someone has put up a sign saying "to let"!'

The sadhu's departure was as sudden as his arrival. All that he had left behind was the sound of his bloodcurdling laughter on my tape recorder, and a few revived animals and birds.

But he did something else. Or, at least, it was what I saw him do that aroused a keen interest in my own mind about bones. As a matter of fact, I became quite passionate about it. One of my rooms had been lying empty. Within a few months, it was filled with the bones and skeletons of dead animals and birds. I read as much as I could about bones. It evoked a strange feeling in my heart to realize that, in the matter of bone structure, no creature on this earth was really that different from any other. We were all basically similar.

I began to feel an odd attraction to the skeleton of whatever being I could find. I even managed to invent a pair of glasses which helped me see straight through the flesh of a living being and look at its skeleton.

It was this fascination regarding bones that led to my curiosity about archaeology and prehistoric animals. Actually, a young south Indian gentleman from Bangalore was responsible for it. His name was Srirangam Deshikachar Seshadri Iyengar—or Mr Iyengar, in short. I met him one day, walking by the river Usri. He was most amiable. Besides, he was a mathematician and a learned man. It was a pleasure talking to him. Over a period of time I got to know him quite well.

It was in his house that, one day, while I was having a cup of tea, I noticed the ankle-bone of an enormous animal. It was kept in a corner of his living room.

I had to go and pick it up. He noticed my interest and said, 'I went to visit a friend in the Nilgiris. He lives on a tea estate. One day, I was just strolling in the area, when I found that bone. I wonder which animal it belongs to? Is it a rhinoceros, or an elephant? Can you tell?'

'No, it's difficult to make a guess,' I replied. But, to myself, I said silently, 'A mathematician you might be. An authority on bones you are not. This bone once belonged to an animal that is neither an elephant nor a rhino. It became extinct several million years ago.'

I could see that the bone came from a brontosaurus. So I decided immediately to visit the Nilgiris.

I began making preparations the same day, and finally got here three weeks ago, with Prahlad in tow. By a remarkable stroke of luck, within four days of our arrival, we found a large number of bones belonging to prehistoric animals in these caves. They were scattered everywhere; it was very difficult to gather them and put them in one place. To tell the truth, if the local adivasis had not given us their sympathy and support, we could not have made headway at all.

As I've said already, this animal, whose bones are now lying in this cave, is unknown to me. I do not believe that any zoologist anywhere in the world will be able to recognize it. Over the next couple of days, I intend to inform Bangalore about my discovery. There is no way that I can remove these bones out of this cave all by myself.

It would be rather nice, if in about a month, a museum in Madras or Calcutta could make room for the skeleton of a prehistoric animal.

*

I am writing my diary in the waiting room of the railway station in Bangalore. What happened yesterday could probably be described far better by a writer than a scientist. But I will do my best to give an accurate description. I have been through many an extraordinary experience, faced grave danger and dealt with terror, but I don't think any of that can compare with my experience yesterday.

Until last evening, I was busy cleaning the bones. It was no easy task to try to remove layers of dust accumulated over so many years. I would clean each bone, as much as I could, and then put it in the right place, with the help of my adivasi assistants. Slowly, the shape and size of the animal began to emerge.

When dusk fell, the adivasis left. I sent Prahlad to the local market to buy vegetables.

I was alone in the cave. It was time to light the petromax. The birds on the peepal tree outside had stopped chirping. There was something rather eerie in the silence.

As I was lighting a match, I heard something scuttle across the floor. A chameleon, perhaps. But when I shone my torch on the floor, I could see nothing.

I lit the petromax and placed it on a flat rock. Instantly, the inside of the cave became brighter.

In that light, I could see the bones, so carefully arranged. Suddenly, it seemed to me as if a faint tremor was running through them. They were no longer still.

Memories of what happened three years ago came back in a flash, making my heart skip a beat. My eyes moved to the mouth of the cave. I could see the peepal tree outside.

That same sadhu was hanging upside down from one of its branches. His left arm was pointing west, his right arm was rotating at enormous speed, his eyes were wide, glittering in the light of the petromax. He was staring straight at me.

Then it started. That same thin, faint, high-pitched voice; the meaningless words, spoken very fast.

An unseen force made me remove my gaze from the sadhu's face, and fix it on the bones of the animal.

It was no longer a skeleton. Under the impact of the sadhu's supernatural powers, it was turning into a colossal prehistoric creature, unknown to man. In just a moment, it would spring to life.

Even at a dangerous moment like this, I did not think of reaching for a weapon. Instead, I just continued to sit still, no different from the lifeless rock that I was sitting on. I did not even think of God, or pray to be saved. The only thing I could think of, was that no one on earth had ever had the chance to witness such a scene, seconds before he died.

I observed every minute detail of the animal's appearance until life returned to its inert limbs. I had gone to such a lot of trouble to reconstruct its skeleton. I was the one who had re-discovered it. When it became alive, would I be the one to be swallowed by the animal, before it attacked anything else?

I darted a quick glance at the sadhu. His face was lit up by a monstrous glee. Once I had used my

knowledge of science on him and tried to steal his mantra. I was even successful, to a large extent, in my attempt. Today, the sadhu was here to pay me back.

A deafening roar boomed through the entire cave, echoing from one end to the other. It froze my blood. The animal had come to life.

Slowly, it raised its gigantic body on its hind legs. A pair of bright green eyes glared at me and the petromax for a few seconds.

Then it began moving forward. The noise it was now making was not a roar, but a low growl. It thrashed its tail on the ground a few times. It seemed agitated, or perhaps frustrated. Then its eyes moved towards the exit and fell on the peepal tree. At once, it shot out of the cave.

The scene that followed will remain etched in my memory until the day I die.

The animal went straight to the tree, grabbed a leafy branch in its mouth and swallowed it. And the sadhu? Could he have known that the end was so near? And could I have imagined that, just before he died, he would give a final magical performance?

When the animal began tugging at the branch, the sadhu nearly slipped off the one from which he was hanging. But, even at such a moment, he was able to raise his left arm, and point it east. Then his right arm began spinning once more, and through his mouth poured a mantra—still incomprehensible, but clearly a different one.

As soon as he finished chanting it, the sadhu lost his hold on the branch and fell with a thud. In the next instant, that massive animal cried out, as if in pain, and keeled over, still clutching a few peepal leaves in its mouth. The sadhu was crushed instantly under its enormous body.

What I saw next was just the opposite of everything I had seen so far. A living, breathing creature, made of flesh and blood, turned once more into a great heap of bones. And through the gaps in its ribs, I could see a human skeleton. The sadhu's body had disappeared in an instant and become a skeleton as well.

A sigh rose from the depths of my heart. Who could avoid the inevitable? That animal was obviously herbivorous, it lived on leaves and plants. When it was brought back to life, it woke up feeling ravenous. Hence its attack on the peepal tree. Had it been a carnivorous animal, no doubt it would have eaten me at once. The sadhu would then have chanted his mantra in reverse and turned it back into a pile of bones, thereby seeking his revenge and punishing me adequately. After that, he would have found another tree and continued to hang upside down.

I had heard the expression 'I have a feeling in my bones', but this experience put a whole new meaning to it!

Prahlad has brought me some tea. It is nearly time for my train. This is where I must stop writing today.

Translated by Gopa Majumdar

Professor Shonku and the Macaw

7 June

Over the past few days, I had been feeling rather low and depressed. This morning, something amazing happened to restore my spirits.

Perhaps I should first explain the reason why I was feeling so morose. A few days ago, another scientist called Gajanan Tarafdar came to see me. He was on his way to Hazaribagh. Having heard my name and read some of my books, he had stopped in Giridih only to meet me and take a look at my laboratory.

This was nothing new, as it happened. Other scientists have visited me before. Many of them, virtually from every country, wish to see my laboratory if they happen to be in India. A Norwegian zoologist once spent a whole month with me. But Tarafdar seemed different from any other scientist with an interest in my work. He asked too many questions, and darted such sharp, restless glances everywhere that it seemed as if he wanted to grasp all the secret details of my research just by looking at things.

Since scientists often work in the same area, there is bound to be a certain amount of rivalry amongst them, to see who has gone further ahead in doing original research and experiments. However, there was no reason to believe that I would answer every question, and reveal everything that I had learnt over the years through my own hard work, using my own intelligence and doing my own calculations. Yet Tarafdar appeared to think that that was exactly what I was going to do. Perhaps it was my meek and mild appearance that led him to harbour such a belief. Or else how did he have the impertinence not only to ask such direct questions, but expect to get answers?

What I was working on at the time, was a potion to make living creatures invisible. I had only had partial success with it. The guinea-pig on which I was using the potion was taking on a hazy, translucent form for seventeen seconds, but was not disappearing completely. Perhaps there was something wrong with one of the ingredients. I was unable to put my finger on it, and was therefore worried and preoccupied. It was during this time of uncertainty that Mr Tarafdar turned up.

I had considerable difficulty in dealing with his barrage of questions. His curiosity was really excessive. He wouldn't stop until he had picked up all the jars and containers in my laboratory, removed their stoppers and smelt their contents. But I noticed one thing, and that amused me a lot. Mr Tarafdar failed to recognize the mixtures and potions that I had made myself. That is to say, he could not guess what ingredients had gone into their composition.

I did not, of course, allow him to handle my notes. Most of the papers that were in my laboratory had references to the formula that I had used to create my 'invisible' potion, and details of all the research that had gone into it. There was one particular notebook that I was guarding carefully from Tarafdar's prying eyes. However, a registered letter arrived while Tarafdar and I were talking. As Prahlad had gone out, I was obliged to leave the room for two minutes to collect the letter. When I returned, I saw that Tarafdar had grabbed that notebook and was devouring every word in it. In his demeanour was a suppressed but intense excitement.

I could not be so rude as to snatch the notebook from his hands. But I was forced to tell him a lie, just to get rid of him. 'Look, I have just received a letter with some bad news,' I told him. 'I cannot talk to you any more, you will have to excuse me.'

Professor Tarafdar returned later, on two occasions. But I did not let him go into my laboratory a second time. The minute I heard of his arrival, I locked the door of the laboratory and asked Prahlad to show him into the living room. On both occasions he had a cup of tea, made small talk, fidgeted a little, and left.

I do not know when he went back to Hazaribagh. Last Wednesday, I received a letter from him. The tone of this letter was most unpleasant. He made some snide remarks about my research and told me that he was not in the least impressed by my work. What was more, he himself was about to invent a magic potion to make things invisible, which would be far better and effective than mine, and *he* would be the one to get all the accolades.

At first, I laughed the whole thing off. Then I had a sudden suspicion. Tarafdar had taken a brief look at my most important notes. Could he have memorized my formula in those few minutes? And was he going to use my own formula to create something more effective? No, surely that was impossible. Tarafdar did not strike me as a brilliant scientist. If anything, his knowledge of science seemed little more than average. Even so, I have to admit that his letter spoilt my mood.

The amazing thing that eventually cheered me up, occurred only today. I had gone for my usual morning walk by the river Usri. When I returned at half past six, I went to look at the flowers in my garden, as I do every day. Suddenly, my eyes fell on the golancha tree in the corner, and were dazzled by a splash of bright colours.

When I got closer to the tree, I found an extraordinary bird perched on a branch, looking steadily at me. It was a macaw—a bit like a cockatoo, but about four times its size. Macaws are usually found in South America. I do not think there is any other bird in the world that is so colourful. Each bird looks as if nature was playing with all the colours in a rainbow when she created it, and decided to paint its body with as many colours as she fancied. A bird like that would light up a whole room, no matter where it was kept.

But how had it found its way to my garden? And

why did it fly down from the tree to settle on my shoulder?

Although it did not belong to me, perhaps it would not mind staying with me for a while, I thought.

I went back to the house with the macaw on my shoulder. Then I arranged for it to remain in my laboratory. Since I spend most of my time there, I thought it would be easier to keep an eye on the bird if it stayed in the same room. For a moment, I did wonder if it might object to the pungent smell from all the chemicals that fill my lab, but the macaw did not utter a single sound in protest.

My cat, Newton, meaowed and hissed a couple of times; but when the bird showed no sign of either annoyance or aggression, Newton calmed down. Perhaps in a few days the two would become friends.

Later in the morning, the bird ate two cream crackers. Then I arranged to feed it properly. Prahlad was quite taken aback at first, but now seems to have accepted its presence. I am sure that quite soon, he will become as attached to the bird as I already am.

When I was working in the laboratory during the day, I couldn't help looking at the bird frequently. Every time I glanced at it, I found it looking straight at me. Who did it belong to? Where had it come from?

19 June

Another extraordinary thing happened today.

I had just taken the guinea-pig out of its cage, placed it on a table and picked up the bottle containing the special potion, when a deep, raucous voice asked, 'What a-r-r-e you do-o-o-ing?'

Startled, I look around quickly. At once, I saw the macaw's beak part and move. 'What ar-r-e you do-o-o-ing? What ar-r-e you do-o-o-ing?' it asked again.

I could hardly believe it. Who knew the bird could talk, and that too, so distinctly? I had never heard such clear speech from any bird before.

All I could do was gape at the macaw. The noise it made next, could only be described as a cackle. I stood foolishly, still clutching the bottle, forgetting to put it down.

The macaw spoke again: 'What is it? What is it? What is it?'

This time, it was my turn to laugh. This bird wanted to know what my bottle contained. The thought was truly amusing.

But the bird began to look a bit stern when it heard me laugh. Then it shot another question at me, its voice sounding sharper than before. 'Why d'you laugh? Why d'you laugh?'

Well, clearly I had to take Mr Macaw seriously, or he would be offended. So I cleared my throat and said, 'There is a medicine in this bottle. Anyone who takes it will become invisible.'

'R-r-r-eally? R-r-r-eally?'

'Yes. If someone were to take it now, he'd disappear for five hours. The time may be decreased or increased by adjusting the amount one takes.'

The macaw remained silent for a few seconds. Then it made a noise that sounded like 'hmm-hmm.' This was followed by one more question: 'What medicine? What medicine?'

I had to hide a smile as I replied, 'I haven't given it a name. But I can tell you what ingredients have gone into it. Extract of gorgonasauce, paranoium potentate, sodium bicarbonate, eggs of a weaver bird, the juice of basil leaves, and tincture of iodine.'

The macaw said nothing. It was staring hard at the floor.

'Where did you learn to speak so well?' I asked.

The bird made no reply. I asked again, 'How did you learn to speak?'

Just for a moment, the bird seemed to part its beak,

but no sound emerged.

I could never have imagined that such a wonderful bird, that I had found purely by chance, would also be able to speak. That was an added bonus.

22 June

Just half an hour ago, I finished my dinner and made my way to the laboratory to lock it up for the night. As I reached the door, I heard someone muttering inside. It was the macaw, but it was speaking softly to itself, repeating the same words over and over. I stopped and listened at the door. The words became clearer: 'extract of gorgonasauce, paranoium potentate, sodium bicarbonate, eggs of weaver bird, juice of basil, tincture of iodine . . .' I heard the same list repeated ten times, before entering the room. Then I cleared my throat and said, 'Good night!'

The macaw stopped its recitation and peered at me for a few seconds. Then it said, 'Buenas noches!' It meant 'good night' in Spanish.

Now there could be no doubt that the bird originally came from South America. When I was locking the door of the laboratory, I could hear it rattling off the list of ingredients again.

I went upstairs, marvelling at the sharpness of this extraordinary bird's memory, and its ability to speak.

24 June

It is a sad day today.

My beloved macaw has vanished. By that, I do not mean that it has become invisible. I did not subject it to any scientific experiment. It just left, as mysteriously as it had appeared.

When I opened the door of my laboratory this morning, I could see at once that the iron rod on which it used to perch, placed by the northern window, was empty. I had grown to trust that bird so completely that I did not even think of tying a chain to its feet.

I could distinctly remember bolting that window. But now it was open. The bird may have somehow slipped through the bars, but who opened the window? Could Mr Macaw have removed the bolt himself, using its large and strong beak? But why? It had seemed happy enough in my house, it was being fed regularly and looked after. So why should it want to escape?

I felt very sad. There was a deep red feather lying on the floor by the window. I picked it up and put it away carefully. Then I locked the laboratory again, and returned to my bedroom upstairs with a heavy heart. I spent the rest of the day sitting in my wicker chair, looking out of the window.

My neighbour, Avinash Babu, came to visit me in the evening. Over a cup of tea, he began to talk such complete nonsense that I felt like dropping one of my new pills into his cup. That would have served him right, but in the event, it proved unnecessary. Perhaps he could see that I was depressed, so he left after a few minutes.

I was feeling extremely unhappy not only because the macaw had disappeared so mysteriously, but because I had really grown attached to it. It had become a friend.

From tomorrow, I must go back to working on my potion. Only hard work can help me forget the pain of losing my friend.

21 July

What happened today is as incredible as it is exciting. I wonder how many scientists have ever had such a thrilling experience.

Recent rains have made the weather turn cool. My walk by the river this morning was most enjoyable. It was probably for this reason, that today I took longer to finish my walk and return home. By the time I did so, it was almost seven. Prahlad, I knew, was out shopping. It was not yet time for him to be back. So, when I got closer to my house and found the front door standing ajar, my suspicions were aroused immediately.

I quickened my pace and reached the door. Prahlad had put a padlock on it when he left. It had not been broken, or unlocked normally. Some scientific method had been used to melt it down.

My heart gave a sudden lurch. I ran into the house.

The first thing I saw was Newton in a corner of the living room, all his hair standing on end. He was looking more like a porcupine than anything else. I could not remember having seen him so tense ever before.

A noise came from the laboratory. It sounded as if someone was in there, rummaging through my papers. I left Newton and ran to the lab. When I arrived at the door, panting, an extraordinary sight met my eyes.

My flasks, beakers, test tubes and all the other apparatus were strewn everywhere. Every bookcase was open, the books and papers scattered on the dusty floor. Some bottles containing chemicals and other liquids were overturned on a table, their contents spilt and dripping over the edge.

In the next instant I saw something else. A sheaf of papers and some notebooks, containing many of my important notes, suddenly rose in mid-air, moved about aimlessly, then made their way to an open window.

The bars on that window had also been melted down. I stared at this spectacle, nonplussed. But that was only for a few moments. Life then returned to my limbs, and I jumped across everything lying on the floor to grab the flying papers.

This was followed by a peculiar struggle. I was thrown into battle with an invisible burglar. He didn't seem to be particularly strong, but I could not see him, and that certainly put me at a disadvantage. Fighting him was not easy, but I refused to give up. Those papers were more precious to me than life itself. They contained the results of all the scientific research that I had carried out over forty years. In a desperate attempt to retrieve them, I threw reckless kicks and punches in the air and, eventually, managed to grab the whole lot. A second later, I could hear my unseen adversary slip through the window and fall on the ground outside. I dragged myself to the window and looked out. A set of footprints was making its way across the lawn, going towards the compound wall.

Then I heard a sound. It was the familiar, raucous voice of a bird, and the flutter of its wings.

The intruder had climbed the wall and was trying to escape. I could guess this as a little sapling of peepal that was peeping out of a crack in the wall was crushed and torn out before my eyes.

At that very moment, a very human voice let out a painful cry.

This was another familiar voice. It belonged to Professor Gajanan Tarafdar.

The invisible macaw had attacked the invisible professor. There were streams of blood sliding down the wall, going towards the grass.

This was followed by a loud thud. Professor Tarafdar had successfully climbed the wall and dropped on the other side. Finally, the sound of running feet reached my ears.

I sank down on the chair by the window, exhausted. My heart was beating very fast.

A faint clang made me look up. The iron rod, on which the macaw used to perch, was swaying a little. Mr Macaw had returned.

'Buenas dias! Buenas dias!' its voice said.

I replied in English, 'Good morning. What's going on?'

'I've come back! I've come back!'

'Yes, I can see . . . sorry, hear . . . that!'

'Thief! R-r-r-obbe-r-r-r, r-r-r-obbe-r-r-r!'

'Who is?'

'Tarr-r-afda-r-r.'

'How do you know Tarafdar?'

In reply to this question, and some others I had to ask, the macaw told me an astounding story.

Tarafdar, it said, had gone to Colombia about a year ago. He stole the macaw from a circus there. Until then, this bird that could speak seventeen different languages and had a fantastic memory, was the property of a magician who worked in the circus. Tarafdar himself could claim no credit for the bird's extraordinary qualities.

After having visited my house, one night he brought the macaw and left it in my garden. The idea was that it would stay with me for a while, learn the formula I was using to make my 'invisible' potion, then return to Tarafdar and repeat the formula to him.

Up to a point, his plan worked. He did learn the formula from the bird, and made a mixture with the same ingredients. This mixture could make a living being vanish for ten hours. Having made it, Tarafdar drank some of it himself and became invisible.

But, before he could disappear from sight, the macaw realized something from his behaviour. It became clear that he was planning to kill the bird, now that it had served its purpose. If it was killed, there would be no danger of it repeating the precious formula to some other scientist. When the invisible Tarafdar opened his wardrobe and the macaw saw a gun being lifted out, it could think of only one way to save itself. Using its beak to remove the stopper on the bottle that contained the mixture, it dipped its beak further in and drank the remaining liquid, thereby making itself invisible as well.

Tarafdar did shoot wherever he could, but succeeded only in hitting and damaging the walls. Then, still invisible, he got into his car and drove from Hazaribagh to Giridih. What he did not realize was that the macaw was travelling with him, as a passenger on the back seat.

When he reached Giridih, he parked his car at some distance from my house. Dawn was about to break at the time. All he then had to do, was hide behind some bushes in my garden and wait until he saw me and Prahlad leave the house. After that, it was just a matter of melting the padlock down and gaining entry.

'Where were you when Tarafdar was stealing my things?' I asked the bird.

'Outside, outside. On your tree!'

'And then?'

'I attacked him, the minute he came out. He's a robbe-r-r-! F-r-r-r-aud!'

'Really? And what about me?'

'You're good, you're good. I will stay here with you, with you!'

'You are most welcome. But I hope you are not friendly with any other scientist? You won't repeat my secret formula to others, will you?'

The macaw cackled loudly.

'When did you swallow that mixture?' I asked.

'At ten last night.'

'I see. In that case, your time is almost up. It's eight now.'

'Yes, yes. I know. Ha ha ha ha!'

Before the traces of its laughter could fade away, I could see the entire laboratory slowly light up. It was not sunlight that was filling my room, but the glorious colours of the macaw's brilliant feathers.

I rose from my chair, dusting the papers and notebooks that I was still clutching in my hands. Then I stroked the macaw's head and said, 'Thank you.'

'Gracias, gracias!' it said in reply.

Translated by Gopa Majumdar

Professor Shonku and the Mysterious Sphere

7 April

Avinash Babu came to my house this morning. He found me sitting in my living room, clutching a newspaper, and said, 'What's the matter? Are you unwell? I don't think I've ever seen you like this before, sitting here doing nothing, so early in the day!'

'The only reason for that,' I replied, 'is simply that I *have* never sat idly like this before!'

'Yes, but why are you being idle now?'

'For over a year and a half, I had been working on building a new machine. This morning, I can finally say that my experiments were successful, and my work is finished. So I have decided to rest for a week.'

Avinash Babu clicked his tongue disapprovingly, shook his head and said, 'How many times have I told you to retire? Surely there is a limit even to the study of science? Or do you mean to say scientists will continue to carry out experiments for ever and ever?'

I smiled a little. 'Yes, that is my belief. There is no end to the questions man wants to ask, you know.'

'I don't know about other men, but it's good to see that you are prepared to stop your questions, at least for the time being. Come on, let's go for a walk.'

Usually, if Avinash Babu turns up when I am busy with my work, it is most annoying. He asks a lot of irrelevant questions, makes snide remarks, and tries to play childish tricks to belittle the seriousness, sensitivity and significance of my work. God knows what he gets out of it all. But he has been my neighbour for nearly twenty-five years, so I put up with him.

Today, as I was not doing anything important, I thought it might not be a bad idea to go out with him. He tries to tease me at times, but I have never had any reason to believe that he wishes me any real harm. So I agreed to go out for a walk.

If anyone suggests a walk in Giridih, one automatically thinks of the riverside. But Avinash Babu began walking in the opposite direction, towards his house. Why? What was he up to?

A few minutes later, he explained the reason himself. 'I found a new toy today. I'll show it to you.'

'A toy?'

'Yes, you'll like it, I am sure, but I am not going to give it to you.'

I made no reply, but said silently to myself, 'You may still be of an age to play with toys, not me!'

On reaching his house, Avinash Babu took me

straight to his living room. There was a glass case in a corner. He opened its door, pointed at something and said, 'Look!'

On the top shelf were a lot of rural handicrafts, ranging from clay figures to animals made of terracotta, trees and birds made of thermocol, a clay tiger from Benaras and heaven knows what else. In the middle of all these knick-knacks was a ball with a plain, smooth surface. It was at this ball that Avinash Babu's finger was pointing.

'How do you like it?' he asked.

It looked like an ordinary ball, but I could not tell what it was made of; nor was it easy to decide what colour it was. Some of it looked earthy, some of it was green, but the rest was a mixture of red and yellow. It looked quite interesting.

Avinash Babu seemed pleased by my interest. 'Where was it made? How did you get it?' I asked.

Avinash Babu replied, 'I do not know the answer to your first question. The second is easy. I was walking by the Usri yesterday, when I saw a dead snake lying on its bank. At first, I only saw the snake, not the ball. It was lying only a few feet away. But when I did, I liked it so much that I picked it up and brought it home. Do you want to hold it in your hand? It is quite heavy.'

Avinash Babu lifted the ball carefully and passed it to me. It *was* rather heavy. And it felt very cold. It was about twice the size of a tennis ball. But, even when I held it in my hand, I could not tell what it was made of. Some of it might be plain clay, but it was probably mixed with something else.

I peered at it, turned it around a couple of times,

then returned it to Avinash Babu.

'Yes, it's certainly quite interesting,' I said. Avinash Babu put it back on the shelf, saying as he did so, 'Hm-hm. So you must admit that other people can also have strange and wonderful things in their possession! Anyway, let's now have that walk. It's a nice day.'

I returned home in a couple of hours, going straight to my laboratory to take another look at my new machine. When the world outside learns about this machine, I have no doubt that I will receive more awards, more recognition.

I have decided to call it a Microsonograph. Noises or sounds, no matter how slight, will be caught by my machine—even those sounds that have either never been heard by human ears, or of whose existence man is totally unaware. Every single sound will be clearly audible through my Microsonograph.

Yesterday, I heard the noise being made by an ant. It was a remarkable experience. It sounded a bit like a cricket's chirp, but it was not steady and monotonous. The noise went up and down, its tone varying from time to time. I think that in time, through this machine, I will be able to learn the language used by ants. And it need not stop there. Every tiny sound made in the natural world is going to be recorded by that machine. It has a knob, which can be moved to change and adjust the wavelength, thereby catching the sound patterns at different levels and different distances.

When I got back home, I set the knob at a particular wavelength and plucked a rose from a bush in a flowerpot. Immediately, a sharp wail, like the strains from a violin, reached my ears through the machine. I could scarcely believe that it was the plant crying out in pain.

Avinash Babu tried to impress me by showing me a strange ball. I wonder how he'd feel if he could hear just a few samples of what my machine can do?

12 April

This morning, just as I was thinking of sending Prahlad over to Avinash Babu's house to invite him to come and look at my microsonograph, the man himself turned up.

His face and the way he was breathing indicated that he was in a state of great excitement. At the time, I had adjusted the wavelength of my machine to that of the grass in my lawn. My gardener was mowing it, and I could hear the joint wailing of all the grass. Avinash Babu entered my laboratory, threw his stick on the table with a clatter, and flopped down on a tin chair. Then he took a deep breath and said, 'Here you are wasting your time on perfectly useless stuff. And over there in my house, such extraordinary things are happening!'

I did not like the note of open contempt in Avinash Babu's voice. Keeping my own voice as grave as possible, I asked, 'What do you mean?'

'Remember that ball I showed you?'

'Yes.'

'It's changing colour every hour.'

'What! How?'

'Well, the colours change ever so slowly. If you stare at it for a few minutes, you won't notice anything drastic. But if you looked at it now, and then went back in a couple of hours and looked at it again, you'll immediately spot the difference. I tell you, I've forgotten everything else. All I've been doing lately is staring at that ball.'

'How was it looking when you left?'

'Much the same as that day when you saw it. Every morning, it looks the same. But, only an hour later, it will look totally different. The most amazing thing starts as dusk falls every evening. The whole ball develops white patches, you see. Then, by midnight, it becomes pure white. It then looks like a giant ball of naphthalene.'

'Remarkable.'

'Perhaps I should inform the press. If I became a little famous because of this mysterious ball, that would be no bad thing, would it? After all, I've never known fame or glory. In fact, maybe I could sell that stuff to the museum in Calcutta and make some money?'

Clearly, Avinash Babu was building castles in the air. But all I said was, 'Before you do all that, shouldn't you investigate the matter? I mean, it could be that the whole thing is either an optical illusion, or may be you are making a mistake somewhere?'

These words seemed to infuriate Avinash Babu. He sprang to his feet, grasped his stick and said, 'Very well, it's all a big mistake. *You* stay right here with all your idiotic experiments. Let me find out how far *my* discovery will take me!'

He stormed out of the room before I could make a suitable reply.

Later in the day however, as it began to get dark, I could not help feeling curious about the ball.

My new instrument, at the time, was giving me a little trouble. Perhaps a connection inside it had become loose. I decided to look into it upon my return, and left for Avinash Babu's house.

I found him leaning over a desk in his living room, writing something with deep concentration. He looked up as I entered and showed me what he had written. 'Does it sound all right?' he asked. 'Here, let me read it out. I have written this for *Anandabazar*: "Dear Sirs, I have recently come into possession of an extraordinary sphere, the like of which I am sure does not exist anywhere else in the world. This sphere has more than one astounding quality. First, it is impossible to work out which metals—or other substances—it is made of (our local scientist, Professor Trilokeshwar Shonku, is of the same opinion). Second, its colour changes every hour, quite spontaneously. Third . . ." Well, how do you like it so far?'

'It sounds fine. What is the third quality?'

'That's what I was in the process of describing. It feels damp at times. That's the third feature. You can see for yourself.'

Avinash Babu left his letter and took me to the same glass case. But this time, I saw him unlock it with a key. 'Touch it,' he told me, 'You will find it damp to the touch. And look, those white patches are back!'

I stretched my right hand and touched the ball. At once, I felt as if an electric shock had run through my body. The reason was simple. The ball was not just damp, but also icy cold.

'Now do you see the difference? Tell you what, why don't you stay a while longer and see all the other changes? Have dinner with me tonight, I'll tell the cook,' Avinash Babu said. The change I had noticed in the ball had quite genuinely aroused my scientific curiosity. If Avinash Babu had not invited me to stay on, I would probably have suggested it myself.

I spent the next five hours in Avinash Babu's house and watched one colour replace another. I have only just got back home. When I left, it was half past eleven. The ball was really looking like a huge, round clump of naphthalene. I wanted to bring it back with me, and keep it in my laboratory for at least a whole day to examine it more carefully. But Avinash Babu would not hear of it. He was determined not to miss this chance to 'out-do' me. His reasoning was simple. I live in Giridih, and so does he. So why should *I* be famous all the world over, and he remain a complete nonentity? It just wasn't fair.

Tomorrow afternoon, I must go back to his house and take another look at that ball.

13 April

Today, Avinash Babu brought the ball to me, wrapped in a towel, and left it here. It is now lying on a table in my laboratory under a glass lid. I spent the whole day watching—to my heart's content—how it changed its colours.

Avinash Babu's arrival was somewhat dramatic. When he entered my laboratory, a little bundle in his hand, there was not even the slightest trace of the enthusiasm I had seen in his face last night. On the contrary, he looked as if he had done something terribly wrong and was suffering particularly strong pangs of remorse.

I had just finished my coffee. Avinash Babu came

in, placed the bundle on a table, wiped his forehead with a corner of his dhoti and said, 'Well, I don't think I can handle this any more. You may keep it. If a reporter comes to my house, I will send him to you.'

Considerably taken aback, I asked, 'What's the matter? What could have happened overnight for you to have such a change of heart?'

'Don't remind me! I've just realized something, you know. This ball has a terrible power, there is evil in it.

A gecko used to live on top of that glass case. This morning it was lying on the floor, dead. But that's not all. I found about a dozen dead cockroaches in that case.'

I could not help laughing. 'What you mean is that ball acted as an insecticide. You should be happy to have found such an effective insecticide, all for free. Why do you sound so sorry?'

'If it killed only insects, I wouldn't worry. I am not feeling very well myself. I feel kind of nauseous.'

'Didn't you say you sat there looking at the ball, day and night?'

'Yes.'

'Does that mean you didn't get enough sleep for two or three days?'

'Yes, it does.'

'Well then, that's the reason why you're feeling sick. It's perfectly clear, isn't it?'

'I don't know . . . may be. Even so, this ball had better stay here with you. I have somehow lost all interest, don't you see?'

I did not tell him what I could see. Avinash Babu did not believe in science. What mattered to him was superstition. He had jumped to the conclusion that the ball had an evil power just because he had seen a few dead insects scattered around it.

His reaction did not surprise me. From my point of view, it would be an advantage to have the ball in my laboratory. So I asked no more questions, and agreed to keep it with me.

It is now half-an-hour past midnight. I have studied the changing colours since eight this morning. In the morning, it was a mixture of earthy green, red and yellow. In the afternoon, the red and yellow faded a little, the green became darker. Towards evening, this dark green gradually gave way to red and orange. Then, as the time for dusk grew nearer, the entire ball became bright red, as if it was a ripe apple.

About seven o'clock, I saw all the brightness fade. The ball began to look grey and dull. At around ten, white patches began to appear on that grey surface.

At this moment, it is dazzling, sparkling white. The electric bulb that is shining on it from the ceiling is of 150 watts. The reflection of that light is making the ball glow even brighter. A haze is forming on the glass lid, a bit like the condensation that comes from ice.

Tomorrow, I will watch the colours again and study their changing patterns. Then, the day after tomorrow, I intend to place it on my work table and carry out a chemical analysis.

14 April

Newton cried and whimpered all night. I have noticed that his mood has changed, almost from the moment Avinash Babu brought the ball to my house. Newton has become far more irritable than I have ever seen him. Throughout the day yesterday, I saw him staring steadily at the glass lid placed over the ball. He looked decidedly put out. Heaven knows why.

Possibly because I didn't get much sleep last night, I woke up this morning with a slight headache. So, before going into the laboratory, I took one of my pills. It is a pill that I have made myself. It cures 277 types of ailments.

The first thing I noticed upon entering the laboratory was that the insects I had collected in little jars were all dead. I had kept them there with a view to hearing and recording the noises they made, with the help of my Microsonograph. Now it was too late.

I had only myself to blame. I knew about the terrible power of the ball, yet I forgot to remove those insects to safety. There was little I could do, except throw the dead insects away and replace the empty jars on the shelf.

Then I looked at the ball, and was reassured to find that its colour was just the same as it had been the previous morning. At least there was no change in the regular pattern. Had the colours altered themselves haphazardly, without following a set routine, my investigation would have become much more difficult.

The inside of the glass lid had steamed up and was covered by droplets. So I lifted it out and was about to wipe it clean, when I heard a noise just outside the door. I wheeled around, and saw Newton poised on the threshold, his back arched, his tail more than double its normal size. His eyes were fixed on the ball.

It became clear instantly that Newton was about to spring up in the air. When he did, I was prepared for him. I moved quickly to stand before the ball, and caught Newton neatly in my arms before he could attack it. Then I carried him outside, left him there and shut the door.

Throughout the remaining time that I spent in the laboratory, I could hear Newton scratching the door. Such violent objection to a mere ball, possibly made chiefly of clay, was extremely mystifying.

*

All day today, I used the Microsonograph to make a chart of the finest natural sounds, normally inaudible to the human ear. Then I recorded those sounds on my tape recorder. Once I finish gathering different kinds of sounds, I will start replaying them and try to understand their meaning. Avinash Babu was saying something the other day about there being a limit to science. He has no idea how much still remains to be learnt, to be discovered.

It is now one o'clock in the morning. I shall now go to bed. But, over the last few minutes, I have been thinking more about the ball than about my machine.

The way those colours change . . . it is an indication of something. I mean, it resembles something I have seen before. But, for the life of me, I cannot place my finger on it. When the ball turns pure white, it appears to be covered with snow. What, then, is the meaning of the other colours? Green, red, yellow, orange—what did they signify? Why do the colours change, in the first place? If *I* cannot work out the reason, who can?

Perhaps tomorrow, when I go back to work, it will all become clear. Maybe it is all quite simple. Sometimes, if one has been puzzling over something quite complex, a relatively easy problem can befuddle one's brain. Perhaps that is what has happened, even to a scientist like me.

I will not think about it any more. Let's see what happens tomorrow.

15 April

Has any other scientist anywhere in the world ever had the kind of varied, horrific and incredible experiences that I have had? I don't know. Sometimes, I feel sorry that I am not a writer. Had I been one, my accounts would have been far more coherent, far more graphic. But then, I am not writing fiction. I am only making entries in a diary, so all I have to do is record all the details in a simple and straightforward manner. Where is the need to worry about the quality of my language? Anyway, let me now try to describe, as clearly and calmly as possible, what happened a short while ago.

Last night, I could not go to sleep when I went to bed after writing my diary. What I had written was that the pattern of the changing colours appeared to hint at something in particular, but I could not see what it was. Tossing and turning in my bed, suddenly I began to see a glimmer of light. I went through the whole pattern again. At midnight, the ball was white. Towards dawn, the white gave way to a glorious mixture of yellow, red and green. As the day wore on, the shades of green grew darker and the other bright colours faded, to give the ball a subdued yet soothing appearance. Then, in the evening, the green changed to red and brown, which was then followed by shades of grey—and later at night, it began to acquire patches of white.

What did these changes remind me of?

I can remember distinctly, the answer to that question flashed through my mind just as the wall clock in the living room struck two.

Those changing colours were remarkably like the changing seasons on this Earth.

The only difference was that what normally took a whole year, was taking place on the ball over just twenty-four hours. At midnight, the ball went through the height of winter when it was covered by snow. Then, towards dawn, yellow, red and green began to appear on its surface, that meant the arrival of spring. As the sun rose higher, spring moved towards summer and the brightness of those colours gradually faded. Early in the evening, when the ball felt damp, that clearly meant that summer was over and it was time for the rainy season. Between sunset and midnight, the rains passed and the ball went through that interim phase between autumn and winter, what we call hemant. Hemant was indicated by those white patches, and then, by midnight, it was winter once more.

Could it be that this ball—this sphere—was a miniature version of our own Earth? Or was it a different planet, where there were changing seasons, there was life and living creatures?

Usually, I never dismiss any idea as 'impossible', but not even in a dream could I have imagined the existence of a planet so small.

I might have continued to think and ponder for a long time, but my thoughts were disturbed by a strange noise. It was coming from downstairs, possibly from my laboratory.

Newton was sleeping in my room. The noise woke him too, and I saw him jump up, pricking his ears. His behaviour made me pick him up in my arms. Then I left my room to go down to the laboratory.

The noise became clearer as I began climbing down the stairs.

'Shonku! Shonku! Shonku!'

Someone was crying out my name, again and again. The word was clear enough, but the voice was not human. Or, at least, it was no ordinary human who was shouting.

As soon as I unlocked and pushed open the door, the sound of that voice intensified by at least four times. And Newton began wriggling in my arms, striving hard to get out. I clutched him tighter, and moved towards the table. The sound was coming from my Microsonograph, not from the ball.

It stopped the second I stepped forward. Then, for about thirty seconds, everything was silent. I could feel Newton trembling violently under my arm.

Then, suddenly, that sharp, piercing screech started again:

'Terratum! Terratum! Speaking from the planet Terratum. Shonku of this Earth! Shonku of this Earth! Can you hear us?'

What could I say? I could hardly believe my own ears!

The question was repeated: 'Can you hear us, Shonku? We are speaking on the same wavelength at which your Microsonograph is set. If you can hear us, please say so. We have a lot to tell you.'

Mesmerized, I replied, 'Yes, I can hear you. What do you want to say?'

The reply came quickly, 'We are prisoners in your room. We know that you have held us here without being aware of it. But what you have done is wrong. We are the smallest planet in the solar system. But that is no reason to dismiss us. There are planets several thousand times larger than your earth, outside your solar system. Our strength lies not in our size, but in our knowledge of science and our intelligence. What you on this Earth have acquired is far, far less than what we have got in our Terratum. We happen to be here today only because we slipped out of orbit. But when we landed on Earth, we fell into a river. That caused us no harm, as we are used to living under the surface of our planet. But what is harmful for us, is this glass lid with which you have kept us covered. We need oxygen to survive, just like you. To tell you the truth, we are not that different from human beings, except that we are much more intelligent, and so small in size that you cannot see us through an ordinary microscope.'

The voice stopped for a few moments. I found myself sitting in a chair. When did I sit down? I had no idea. Then the voice resumed speaking.

'We have only one request for you. Please remove that lid. We are already feeling weak. If we die, you will be responsible for the death of a whole planet, and you will have to carry that load of guilt all your life. Do you think you can do that? Please listen to us. Release us, please. You are a scientist. Do you not feel any sympathy for us?'

There was a question in my mind, struggling to get out. Now I couldn't help asking it. 'Do you have the power to kill creatures that may be far bigger than you?'

There was no immediate reply. I went on, 'Answer me. In the last few days, all living creatures that went near you died. Are you responsible for their death?'

This time, another question was thrown at me. 'Do

you know what a virus is?'

'Of course!'

'All right. What is a virus?'

Such a stupid question was most insulting, but I made my reply. 'It is a germ that can cause an infectious disease.'

'Correct. What is the size of a virus?'

'It is visible only under a microscope.'

'Right. But are you aware that these small germs can wipe out the population of an entire city?'

'Why just a city? An entire nation may be wiped out. Who hasn't heard of epidemics?'

'Yes. Now do you see where our strength lies?'

'Do you spread germs? Viruses?'

'Spread? No, we don't have to spread anything.'

'What do you do then?'

Again, there was no reply. Suddenly I realized that my shirt was wet with perspiration. In my mind, a terrible suspicion raised its head. Was each inhabitant of this new planet itself a virus? If that was the case, they could attack the whole world and finish it . . .

'. . . in three months,' said the voice.

I gave a start. Were those words uttered in reply to a question? But I hadn't spoken at all.

Now I could hear laughter. It was faint, but filled with infinite contempt. Then some more words followed. 'We can read your thoughts. You are wondering, aren't you, if we have the power to spread illness and disease everywhere in the world? Yes, we have. In just three months, we can empty the world of its human population. An epidemic does not call for hard work. Only one of us is enough to kill everyone in Giridih.

And if all of us were to get together . . .'

The voice appeared to be growing faint. Was it the fault of my machine?

'No, your machine is working perfectly,' the voice answered my unspoken question. 'It is we who are getting weaker every minute. If you don't lift that lid and let some fresh air in, we are all going to die. Who will be responsible for our death? You, Professor Trilokeshwar Shonku! No one will arrest you for this mass murder, but surely you have something called a conscience? How can a scientist be so cruel? Think, Shonku, just think . . . !'

'If I let you live, and release you, will you promise not to attack anyone on this Earth? Will you stop your vengeful thoughts? How can I trust you?' I asked.

No one answered this question. After a few minutes' silence, through my machine came a horrible chorus. This time, several voices were crying together. I could not tell how many voices had joined the first, but there could be no doubt that each was screaming; and the note of intense agony that each voice held was unmistakable.

'Shonku! Shonku!'

My name rose above the sound of all the crying and wailing.

'Shonku! Shonku! Shonku!'

'Yes?'

'Remove that lid, *now*! We are about to die. You can save our lives. Do not become a killer. All your life, your conscience will . . .'

The voice grew fainter, and fainter.

*

I continued to sit in my chair. My mind was in complete turmoil and filled with great anxiety, but I knew where my duty lay. I could not remove that glass lid. I could not put at risk the lives of all the people on this Earth, just to save those who lived in a planet called Terratum.

No words came from my Microsonograph. All I could hear was that piercing scream. It went on for some time, then became one long wail. Then there were broken sobs. And then nothing.

Every sound faded away to leave complete silence. I waited for another minute before switching my machine off.

Then I slowly walked over to the ball and lifted the lid. The clock was striking the hour. It was 5 a.m. But today, the colours of spring had failed to appear on Terratum. It looked grey and dull.

I picked it up and glanced at Newton. He, too, was staring at the ball. However, there was no hint of aggression in his look. 'Do you want to play with this ball? Go ahead!' I said.

I placed the ball on the floor. Newton came forward. Then he struck it with his front paw. At once, the smallest planet in the solar system broke into several pieces and lay scattered on the floor.

Translated by Gopa Majumdar

Professor Shonku and Chee-Ching

18 October

This morning, I had just left my bed, washed my face and was about to go to my laboratory, when Prahlad came to me and said, 'There's a gentleman to see you. He's waiting in the living room.'

'Did you get his name?'

'No, babu. He spoke in English. He looks like a Nepali.'

I went to meet my visitor. He turned out to be a Chinese-looking man, wearing a long, loose brown overcoat. If he *was* Chinese, then he was the first visitor from China to set foot in my house.

The man rose to his feet as he saw me come in, flung aside the cane he was clutching in his hand, and bowed deeply from his waist. I said, 'namaskar', invited him to sit down and asked him why he had come to see me.

My question seemed to cause him a great deal of amusement. He chuckled like a child, shook his head from side to side and said, 'Ha ha ha ha . . . you folget, you folget. Bad memoly, bad memoly!'

Bad memory? Forget? Had I met this man before? How could I have forgotten? My memory wasn't that bad, surely?

The Chinese allowed himself to enjoy my confusion and embarrassment for several minutes. Then, abruptly, he took out a red wooden ball from his coat pocket, held it in front of my nose, and twirled the ball with his right hand. He did this only three or four times before the red ball became white. He twirled it once more, and it became black. Almost at once, I could remember—very clearly—the events of a particular evening four years ago.

This man was the magician, Chee-ching, from Hong Kong!

There were reasons why I had failed to recognize him. To start with, the difference in appearance between one Chinese and another is only slight. Besides, the circumstance and atmosphere under which I had seen him in Hong Kong were entirely different from that in my house in Giridih. He was dressed differently, too. That day, in Hong Kong, Chee-ching was performing on a stage, wearing a dazzling green, red and black silk robe. On his head was a striped, conical hat.

The trick he showed me using that wooden ball, made every memory of that evening come flooding back, as if I was watching pictures on a screen.

I was on my way to Kobe in Japan, to join a conference of physicists. I had stopped in Hong Kong to spend a couple of days with an American friend called Benjamin Hodgkins.

Hodgkins was a scientist. He was over sixty years old. But that did not stop him from going out and having fun. He took me to Chee-ching's show the day I arrived.

I enjoy magic shows largely because I get a childish pleasure out of seeing through a magician's clever ploys. But I can appreciate, just as much, a magician's intelligence and imagination if I see something totally original. Magic that claims to be sophisticated and at a high level has to turn to science for help. A magician has to know enough about physics, chemistry, physiology, psychology, everything.

Chee-ching, I was told, was a well-known magician. This made me quite curious, so I could not refuse Hodgkins's invitation.

Chee-ching pulled off quite a few tricks, using sleight of hand, light and shadow, gadgets and instruments, even chemicals. All were enjoyable. However, when he began hypnotizing people from the audience, suddenly the whole thing became objectionable. He picked some meek and mild-looking men, invited them up on the stage and proceeded to make fun of them in various ways. One man chewed a ball of wool for five minutes, convinced that it was an apple. Another man thought the handle of a chair was his pet dog, and stroked it lovingly. When they came out of their trance and found the rest of the audience laughing uproariously, they looked really pathetic.

I said to Hodgkins, 'I don't like this. Have these

men paid good money just to be insulted?'

Hodgkins replied, 'What can anyone do, tell me? If they go up on the stage quite willingly, how can you blame the magician?'

I was trying to think of a way whereby Chee-ching could be stopped, when I realized that everyone in the audience was looking at me. What was going on?

I looked at the stage, and found Chee-ching smiling and pointing a finger at me. When he caught my eye, he said, 'If you don't mind, sir, can you come up here for a minute?'

Obviously, my appearance had prompted the magician to think that I too, was simple and timid. I was already looking for a chance to teach him a lesson, and that chance had now fallen into my lap. So I went up on the stage, feeling quite pleased.

Chee-ching spent the next half an hour trying to put me under a hypnotic spell. He swung a luminous pendant in front of my eyes, ran his fingers over my eyelids, switched all the lights off except one that shone on his own face while he stared hard at me, chanted a lot of gibberish in a monotonous sing-song tone . . . in short, he tried every trick that he could possibly think of. But none of it worked. He failed to influence me in any way, and I remained as alert as ever.

In the end, sweating profusely, he gave up, though he did not directly admit defeat. He left me, and addressed the audience. 'Sorry, I made a mistake, it is my own fault,' he said, his voice filled with contempt. 'The man being hypnotized has to have a brain. I did not know that this gentleman does not possess such an object!'

Perhaps such a remark was adequate to cover up his embarrassment. Perhaps the audience forgave him. But I could only imagine what must have been going through his own mind.

I left Hong Kong for Japan the following day. When I stopped in Hong Kong again on my way back, Chee-ching was not there. I was told that he had gone to perform in Australia.

That was four years ago. Now, he had suddenly

turned up at my house. Why? What could be the reason behind his visit?

Chee-ching spoke before I could ask him.

'You Plofessol Shonku?'

I nodded.

'You scientist?'

'Yes, so it would seem!'

'Science is magic.'

'Yes, you might say that. It *is* a kind of magic.'

'And magic is science. No? Ha ha ha ha!'

Chee-ching was laughing a lot. If I didn't laugh with him, it might appear rude. So, this time, I joined him.

'You work here?' he asked, still pronouncing every 'r' as an 'l'.

'Yes, I work here.'

I took him to my laboratory. Chee-ching saw the instruments I had invented, the medicines I had made and all the apparatus I used, and seemed suitably impressed. 'Wongaful! Wongaful!' I heard him exclaim several times.

Then he noticed three large bottles filled with a liquid. 'Water?' he asked.

I smiled. 'No,' I said, 'those bottles contain acid. Strong and dangerous acid.'

'Acid? Very nice, very nice!'

Why did he think acid was 'nice'? I couldn't understand.

Having finished the tour of my laboratory, he sat down in a chair, wiped his face with a purple handkerchief, and said, 'You are great!'

I saw no point in protesting just to appear modest,

since many important people all over the world, had already called me 'great', long before Chee-ching did.

'Yes, you are great. But I am greater,' he added.

What! What was the man saying? He was just a professional magician, making money by pulling the wool over people's eyes . . . and he thought he was 'greater' than *me*? What extraordinary powers did he have that other magicians didn't?

The question rose to my lips, but I didn't utter it.

Prahlad had served us coffee. Now I saw Chee-ching lift his cup, but his eyes went to the ceiling and he began staring at something specific. I followed his gaze and looked up. As soon as I did, he said, 'Lizard.'

On the ceiling, close to a beam, lay sprawled an old inhabitant of my laboratory—a gecko.

'Do you know what it's called in Bengali? We call it a tiktiki,' I told him.

Chee-ching dissolved into giggles once more. 'Tikitiki? Ha ha. Very nice. Tikitiki.'

He finished his coffee in two long gulps and stood up. He had a show in Calcutta the same evening, so was in a hurry to get back, he said. He had come to Giridih only to meet me.

When he had gone, I pondered for several minutes on the possible reason for his visit, but got nowhere.

19 October

I was working in my laboratory this afternoon, when Newton came in and jumped up on my table. Normally, he never does such a thing. My table is almost always piled high with the apparatus and gadgets that I use, as well as chemicals. Newton had jumped on that table only once, soon after he came to my house. I had reprimanded him and, since then, he had never disobeyed me. Today, I was considerably taken aback to see him ignore my instructions.

Then, just as I was about to say something sternly, I found him staring at the ceiling, like Chee-ching.

I looked up at once. There was nothing unusual. The same gecko was still sprawled on the ceiling. Newton had seen that gecko dozens of times before, and never displayed any emotion. Why, then, was he looking at it so sharply, and why had all the hair on his body risen?

I decided to lift him off the table. But he hissed so viciously as soon as I laid a hand on his back that I felt positively shaken. Could it be that a cat had spotted something in that gecko that human eyes could not see?

I took out the binoculars I keep in a drawer and peered at the gecko through them. Didn't it look slightly different? Were those reddish, semi-circular marks on its back always there? And that tinge of yellow in its eyes . . . had I noticed it before? Perhaps not. But then, until now, there had been no need to peer so closely at a gecko.

The insect began to move, so I took my eyes from the binoculars. The gecko scuttled down to the wall from the ceiling, then swiftly disappeared behind the cupboard that contains all my jars and bottles.

Newton calmed down instantly, possibly because he could no longer see the gecko. He jumped down on the floor and left the room, purring softly, to go outside on the veranda. I stopped worrying about the gecko and returned to my research work.

What I was trying to do, was invent a substance which could be turned into small pills. If someone kept such a pill in his pocket, he would be able to feel cool in the summer, and warm in winter. In other words, my invention could be called an 'Air-conditioning pill'.

*

My servant, Prahlad, has been working for me for almost thirty years. He never touches any of my apparatus in the laboratory. I get very few visitors. Those who come do not go into the laboratory, unless they are scientists, and I accompany them myself.

When I am not in the lab, the door is always locked. The windows are bolted from inside. Last night, when I left the room, the three bottles filled with various dangerous acids were all full, almost to the brim. I saw this with my own eyes.

Now, however, when my eyes happened to fall on them, I could see that the one on the left, containing carbodiabolic acid, was half empty.

There was no chance of the acid evaporating through the night. The bottle had no cracks through which some of the acid might have leaked out on the table and dried. Where, then, had it gone? All three acids were so powerful that if anyone handled them without sufficient care, he was bound to die.

I stopped working and pondered over this. But nothing made any sense. I needed all three acids. Without them, I just could not proceed with my experiments.

I was debating what to do next, when a slight noise made me glance at the cupboard. A creature was peering out from its top.

It was that same gecko, but it would be wrong to call it by that name for there were now marked changes in its appearance. Its eyes were almost wholly yellow, the black pupils had virtually disappeared. They appeared to be burning like yellow flames. There was nothing soothing in those eyes.

Its nose seemed different, too. The nostrils were much larger than before. Its skin was once a mixture of pale green and yellow. Now its whole body was covered by those red, semi-circular marks. If I hadn't already known about the existence of a gecko in my laboratory, I would have assumed that this creature was a new species of reptile.

The gecko gazed steadily at me for a while, then it breathed noisily through its nose. It sounded like a faint hiss. I could hear it clearly. And there was one more thing. The gecko seemed longer and larger in size.

Even as I was staring at it, it looked away and fixed its eyes on the table. Then it inched its way to one corner of the cupboard and appeared to be lying in wait for something. A second later, suddenly, it sprang in the air and landed on my table. All the apparatus on it, some made of glass, shook and clattered in protest.

The distance between the table and the cupboard was at least ten feet. Such a huge long jump was so unexpected that, for a few moments, I just stood still like a statue.

Now I could watch the gecko more closely. Its tail, though longer, seemed unchanged. But its head, nose, eyes, even skin, were all different. Between its eyes, near the top of its head, I noticed something protruding, like a horn. And its claws were abnormally sharp and large. The gecko was staring straight at the bottles filled with those acids. Then it opened its mouth and flicked its tongue. Its tip was forked, like the tongue of a snake.

What followed was so completely incredible, that I could do nothing but gape. The gecko scurried over to the half-empty bottle of carbodiabolic acid, climbed to its top, and slipped its whole body into the bottle, using only its hind feet and claws to grasp the sides of the bottle, so that it did not lose its balance. Then I saw it drink the remaining liquid—that terrible, lethal acid—with every appearance of nonchalance.

As it drank, its tail, hanging out of the bottle, grew larger to match the rest of the body. As soon as I saw that happen, a word escaped through my lips: 'Dragon!'

It was a Chinese dragon.

That old, familiar gecko, that was almost like a pet, had turned into a dragon today; and its favourite drink seemed to be a lethal acid!

I could hardly believe my eyes. But, perhaps because I am a scientist, I wanted to see more, even when something so perfectly amazing . . . almost supernatural . . . was taking place inside my own room. I had to see what might happen next. What did happen was this, the gecko—now turned dragon—came out of the bottle and, instantly, became twice its already enlarged size. I noticed smoke coming out of its nostrils as it breathed.

Then it made its way to the second bottle. It contained nitroannihilin acid. This time, it didn't have to climb the bottle to get to its top. All it had to do was raise itself on its hind legs, grasp the bottle's neck with its front feet and remove the stopper with its teeth. In just a few seconds, it finished every drop. Then it grew further in size.

As it began moving towards the third bottle, suddenly a voice spoke in my head. 'Enough!' it said. 'This creature has to be stopped. Never mind if it drinks acid. Surely a scientist like you can find a way to deal with it?'

I did not waste another second. In a safe kept in the corner lay my electric pistol, my most powerful weapon. I ran and took it out. It was easy enough to use. If I took aim and shot a living being, a shock of 400 volts would pass through its body. It could not hope to remain living after that. I had created the pistol, but had never had any reason to use it. Today, I was going to test its strength on this dragon.

The dragon, by this time, had reached the bottle filled with phorosatanic acid, and had removed its stopper. I crept closer, took aim and pressed trigger. At once, bright electric light shot out like a stream of bullets and hit the dragon's shoulder. It was strong enough to kill an elephant. But, to my complete amazement and horror, I saw that the electric shock had done absolutely no harm to the dragon, which had grown even bigger, and now measured something like four feet. When the electric shock hit its body, all it did was give a slight shudder. Then it left the bottle, turned its head and stared straight at me through its glowing yellow eyes, for nearly ten seconds.

I could feel my limbs go numb. Then the dragon breathed again, making a hissing noise. This time, clouds of red smoke came out of its nostrils as it breathed, That poisonous, sharp, acrid smoke began to envelop all my senses, blurring my vision.

Just before I lost consciousness, I saw the dragon attack all that was kept on my table. Under its stamping feet and swishing tail, all the equipment and apparatus was breaking, crushing, crumbling . . . being totally destroyed.

*

It was the sound of Prahlad's voice that brought me round. 'Babu! Babu!' he was shouting.

I opened my eyes and sat up quickly, to find myself seated in a chair in my laboratory. Prahlad looked quite remorseful. 'Sorry, babu. I didn't know you had fallen asleep!' he said.

'What's the matter?'

'That Nepali man. He left his stick behind, didn't he?'

'Stick?'

My eyes went to the door. Chee-ching was standing there, a big smile on his face. 'This time, I folget my stick. Vely solly!'

'But the dragon?' I blurted out.

'Dagon? You see dagon?'

'All my equipment . . . my gadgets . . . !'

The words died on my lips. To my total embarrassment, I saw now that everything on my table was exactly as it had always been. Nothing had moved, nothing was broken.

But the acids? All three bottles were empty.

I was staring at these, wide-eyed, when Chee-ching started giggling again.

'Hee hee hee! A little magic—but great magic! Look, there's your dagon!'

Chee-ching pointed at the ceiling. I looked up, and found the same little gecko back in its place.

'And your acid!'

This time, I glanced at the bottles and, before my own eyes, each filled up, right up to its brim, with a clear liquid.

Chee-ching now folded his hands like an Indian. 'Nomoskal, Plofessol Sonku,' he said. Then he left.

I could hear Prahlad muttering to himself, 'I thought I could use that stick. A very nice stick it was, too. But that babu was so quick to come back. Why, it's barely five minutes since he left the first time!'

PS 19 October

I opened my diary to record my experience with the dragon, but discovered that it had already been written, in my own handwriting. Was this another sample of Chee-ching's astounding magic?

Translated by Gopa Majumdar

Professor Shonku and the Little Boy

7 September

Something rather interesting happened this morning. I was working in my laboratory, when Prahlad came in and said there was someone to see me. When I asked, 'Who is it?' Prahlad began scratching his head. 'He did not give me his name, babu', he replied, 'but he is not like the men who usually visit you.'

'Do I really have to see him? I am rather busy right now.'

'Well, he said it was very important. He won't go without seeing you.'

There was little I could do after this. So I stopped working and went to meet my visitor.

It turned out to be a man of about thirty, very simple and ordinary in appearance. He was wearing a somewhat dirty dhoti, two of the buttons on his bush shirt were missing, and the stubble on his face was at least three days old. He was standing just outside the front door, his hands folded in a 'namaskar'. He looked very meek and mild.

I asked him why he had come to see me. The man swallowed before replying. 'Er . . . if you could kindly come to my house, sir, I'd be very grateful.'

'Why, what's the matter? I am quite busy, you see.'

The man grew even more apologetic. 'Yes, but who else can I go to? I live in Jhajha. My little boy is ill . . . I can't even tell what's wrong with him. You are the most famous doctor in this area, so I came to you.'

It was very difficult not to laugh. But I managed to hide a smile and said, 'I'm afraid you've made a mistake. I am not a doctor, but a scientist.'

The man now looked like a pricked balloon. 'Mistake? You're a scientist? Oh, then of course I've made a mistake. But . . . who will help me now?'

'Why, you have doctors where you live, don't you?'

'Yes, but they couldn't help.'

'What's wrong with your son? How old is he?'

'He was four last June. We call him Khoka at home, his real name is Amulya. What happened, you see . . . only the other day . . . I mean, last Wednesday, Khoka slipped and fell in our courtyard. One corner of it is quite mossy, and has become slippery. Khoka hurt his head, on the left side. He cried quite a lot, and then I noticed a large swelling over that area. But that swelling went down in a couple of days . . . but since then, my little boy has been talking complete nonsense. He's never talked like that before. None of us can understand a word. Yet it seems as if those words have meanings, they are not just gibberish. But I haven't had much education, I'm only a clerk in a post office. What do *I* know about anything?'

'Couldn't the doctors who saw your son follow his words?'

'No, sir. But then, they are ordinary doctors, none of them is well known or anything. So I thought I'd come to you.'

'I happen to know Dr Guha Majumdar in Jhajha. He's a good doctor.'

At this, the man began to look even more pathetic. 'Yes, but I haven't got enough money to call a big doctor home, have I? Everyone said, go to Dr Shonku in Giridih. He's a kind man, he'll treat your son and cure him. And he won't charge a paisa, either. So that's why I am here.'

I felt very sorry for the man. So I took out twenty rupees from my wallet and gave it to him. 'Get Dr Guha Majumdar. I am sure he will be able to help,' I said.

The man took the money and put it in his pocket, looking both relieved and grateful. Then he folded his hands. 'I must go now. I am so sorry to have disturbed you. Please forgive me.'

When he had gone, I heaved a sigh of relief and returned to my laboratory. How could the local people think I was a doctor? The thought was as amazing as it was amusing.

10 September

It is a long-standing habit of mine to get up before sunrise. I wash my face, and then I go for a walk by the river. This morning was no exception. When I returned after my walk, I found Dr Pratul Guha Majumdar from Jhajha waiting in my living room, together with the same man who had visited me three days ago. I felt perfectly taken aback. Dr Guha Majumdar is usually quite cheerful, but today he was looking solemn and worried. He rose as he saw me come in and said 'namaskar'. Then he added, 'You might be happy to pass this case on to me, Professor Shonku, but I find it impossible to treat this patient.'

I called Prahlad and told him to bring some coffee. Then I sat down on a sofa and said, 'What's the matter with this boy? What's he suffering from? Is he in pain?'

'No, he does not appear to be in any pain or discomfort.'

'So what is it? Has he damaged his brain because of that fall? Is he delirious?'

'I don't know. He is talking quite a lot, but so far I haven't heard him say anything that can be dismissed as mere raving or ranting. Some of what he's been saying is totally correct, amazingly so.'

'But what can I do in this matter, tell me?'

The doctor and the boy's father exchanged a look. Then the doctor said, 'Come with us and see the whole thing for yourself. We can go in my car. If nothing else, you will find the case remarkable and interesting. Frankly, if anyone can do anything to help, it has to be you.'

I knew the doctor would not have made such a request without good reason. So I had to agree to accompany them. We travelled in the doctor's Fiat and reached Jhajha in a couple of hours.

On the way there, I learnt that the boy's father was called Dayaram Bose. He had been working as a postal clerk in Jhajha for the last seven years. His family consisted of his wife and his only son called Amulya, alias Khoka.

The appearance of Mr Bose's house was in keeping with its master's. It had only two rooms and a thatched roof. The courtyard, where Khoka had fallen, was small. We found Khoka lying in a small cot in one of the two rooms, his head resting on a pillow. His body was thin, but his head and eyes were big. His hair had been cut very short.

He saw us enter the room and said, 'Swagatam!'

I smiled in reply. 'Where did you learn to greet your guests in Sanskrit?' I asked. Khoka did not answer my question. Instead, he stared at me for a few seconds and said, 'Six and seven point two five?'

His English accent was perfectly clear, but what did such a question mean? I looked at Mr Bose and said, 'Where did he learn all this stuff?'

The doctor replied instead of Mr Bose. 'As far as I can make out,' he whispered, 'no one has taught him to say anything. He is saying everything entirely on his own. That's where the problem lies, you see. Otherwise, his behaviour is quite normal. He is eating normally, but may be he is sleeping a little less. We left here at five. He was already up and talking to himself.'

'What was he saying so early in the morning?' I wanted to know.

This time, the answer came directly from Khoka: 'Corvus splendens, Passer domesticus.'

There was a chair behind me. I sat down on it very

quickly. Khoka had just told me the Latin names of two different birds—birds we are all familiar with. In fact, those are the two birds that begin a chorus every morning, before any other. A crow is Corvus splendens and a sparrow is Passer domesticus.

Now I turned to Khoka. 'Can you tell me who taught you these names?' I asked gently. Khoka did not reply. He was gazing steadily at a gecko on the wall. I tried again. 'You said something to me a few minutes ago. What was it? What did you say?'

'Six and seven point two five.'

'Yes, but what does that . . . ?' I broke off, as I suddenly remembered that the numbers related to the power of my spectacles: minus six and minus seven point two five.

Never before had I had such a remarkable experience. I moved towards the bed and leant over Khoka. 'Can you tell me, doctor, exactly where on his head the swelling came up? Where was he hurt?'

Khoka answered me before the doctor could open his mouth. 'On the Os temporal,' he said calmly.

This was absolutely incredible. This little boy had even learnt the medical name for a bone in his head. He was only four years old!

I decided to take Khoka to my own house and keep him under observation. Perhaps it would help me to make a study of how the human brain worked. As a scientist, I might gain a lot from the experience.

Mr Bose and the doctor both agreed to let Khoka go with me. Only Khoka's mother said, 'All right, you may take him with you, but please bring the old Khoka back to me. I want him the way he was. A four year old should have the brain of a four year old, shouldn't he? What he's been saying of late has really been to himself, not to us. We can't understand a word, anyway. It seems to me as if it isn't our boy who lives with us, but someone else. I find that very painful. He's our only child, please do remember that, doctor.'

I didn't know the cure for Khoka's 'ailment', either. Yet how could I tell myself that even a scientist like me could not possibly find a solution to the problem, if I applied my brain to it? Of course, a major question that had to be tackled was, whether or not Khoka's symptoms could be described as signs of an illness. What was obvious was that his parents were distressed, as anyone would be if their little son's behaviour changed overnight, quite inexplicably.

We left Jhajha at around half past eleven. Dr Guha Majumdar took us back to Giridih. We had covered about twenty-seven miles when the car suddenly came to a stop. Khoka simply said, 'Sparking-plug.' When the bonnet was opened, we discovered that our sparking-plug wasn't working properly. When that problem was fixed, the car started again and gave us no further trouble. Khoka remained silent throughout the remaining journey.

*

He has been with me since yesterday. I have put him in a room on the first floor that faces south. He seems totally at ease. Not once has he mentioned his parents or his own home. When he heard that my cat was called Newton, he said, 'Gravity'. Somehow, he had learnt about Sir Isaac Newton's discovery of the force of gravity.

Most of the time, Khoka just lies in his bed and seems lost in thought. Prahlad is very happy to have a child in the house. He stays with Khoka during the time when I have to attend to other work. The only thing that disappoints Prahlad is that Khoka does not talk to him. When Prahlad mentioned this to me, all I could say was, 'A few more days here might help him to get back to normal.' As soon as the words left my mouth, I couldn't help wondering if there was any truth in what I had just said.

At two o'clock this afternoon, I dissolved a sleeping pill in a glass of milk and gave it to him, in the hope that it might calm and soothe his brain. Khoka took the glass from me and said instantly, 'Somnolin.' The pill had no smell at all, and it was impossible to tell just by looking at the milk that it was mixed with anything. But Khoka had caught me out, so there was no point in lying. 'It is to help you sleep. You'll feel better after a good sleep. Drink your milk,' I told him.

Khoka replied calmly, 'No. Do not give me any drugs. Don't make that mistake.'

'How do you know I am making a mistake? Can you tell me what's wrong with you?'

This time, Khoka said nothing. He just stared out of the window. I went on, 'Are you ill? Do you know the name of the disease?'

Khoka remained silent. Heaven knows if he will ever give me an answer to that question. I will have to do a lot of reading myself and try to find the truth.

11 September

From this morning, Khoka's knowledge about most things seems to have grown tenfold.

I spent a long time yesterday going through a lot of medical and scientific books, but could get nowhere near learning anything about Khoka's strange 'illness'. In the afternoon, I was in my study upstairs, reading a huge tome on brain diseases, when suddenly I heard Khoka's voice. 'You won't find anything in there!' he told me.

Startled, I raised my eyes to find him standing before me. I had no idea that he had left his room. Until that moment, he had shown no interest in leaving his own room.

I shut the book. Khoka's tone held a note of such authority that there was no way I could ignore it. If an old man of sixty had told me that a book written by an eminent scientist did not contain the information I needed, I might not have believed the man. But a few words spoken by a four-year-old child instantly made me put the book away.

Khoka paced up and down for a while. Then, suddenly, he turned around to face me, and said, 'Terrinium Phosphate.'

How extraordinary! How did Khoka know the name of the new acid I had made? It was kept in my laboratory downstairs. 'It's a very strong acid,' I said to him.

For the first time, there appeared to be a hint of a smile on Khoka's face. 'I want to see your lab,' he said simply.

Oh no! I had no wish to take him there. In his present frame of mind, he should not be anywhere near those potent acids and gases. Heaven knew what he might do when he saw them. After a few seconds of indecision, I finally said, 'What will you do there? It's full of dust, and it smells pretty foul. There are some awful chemicals in there.'

Luckily, Khoka said nothing and resumed his pacing. Then he found a globe on my table, and began twirling it. The paint on it had worn off over a portion near South America. Some of the names had therefore disappeared completely. Khoka stared at that bald patch for a few moments, then picked up a pen from my desk and proceeded to scribble something on the globe. When he finished, I took out a magnifying glass and peered over what he had written in minute letters. The words were Salvador, Jacobina, Campo Belo, Itabuna. Those were the names that had been missing.

After that, Khoka began talking again and went on all day. He mentioned Einstein's equation, my own Polar Riplean theory, told me which valley on the moon was the biggest, which mountain was the highest, why there was so much carbon dioxide in the atmosphere of Mercury. He even told me what germs were flying around in the air in my own room! In between giving me all these pieces of information, he took some time off to sing an entire Carnatic raga and recite a whole passage from Shakespeare's *Hamlet*, starting with 'To be or not to be . . . !'

Around 4 p.m., I asked Prahlad to sit with Khoka and went to my room to finish some work. Prahlad happened to fall asleep. When he woke, he couldn't find Khoka anywhere in the room. So he came running to me, and we rushed downstairs to look for him. Khoka had clearly slipped downstairs while Prahlad was asleep, for we found him trying to push open the locked door of my laboratory, and peering through a little crack.

I did not scold him. All I did was grab his hand and say, 'Let's go and sit in the living room.' He came with me like an obedient child and sat down on a sofa. At that moment, my neighbour Avinash Babu turned up.

I did not welcome his arrival. Avinash Babu loves spreading gossip. If he saw Khoka and realized that this little boy was very different from any other, he would go and tell the whole town. Naturally, everyone would then wish to meet this extraordinary child, and my house would turn into a fair ground, its chief and only attraction being Khoka.

Needless to say, Avinash Babu was very surprised to find Khoka on the sofa. 'Hey, where did *he* come from? I don't think I've ever seen him in Giridih!' he exclaimed.

'He's come to stay with me for a while,' I said quickly, 'His father's my cousin.'

Avinash Babu tapped Khoka's cheek lightly, as one does sometimes with small children, and asked, 'What's your name, dear boy, eh?'

Khoka stared solemnly at him for a few seconds. Then he simply said, 'Ectomorphic cerebratonic.'

Avinash Babu gave a start and widened his eyes. 'Oh my God, what kind of a name is that, Mr Professor?' he gulped.

I smiled. 'That's not his name, Avinash Babu. What he just said is a scientific description of your physical appearance and behaviour. His real name is Amulyakumar Bose, but everyone calls him Khoka.'

'A scientific description?' Avinash Babu still sounded

totally taken aback. 'Are you now drilling your own theories into tiny tots?' he mocked.

I would probably have ignored this jibe and remained silent, but Khoka made a reply before I could say anything. 'He hasn't taught me a single word,' he declared, and refused to speak any more.

Avinash Babu's face grew a little grave. He left soon afterwards, without having a cup of tea or coffee. His demeanour made me afraid. It seemed pretty obvious that he would spread the news about Khoka. If too many people began disturbing us, I'd have to tell the police. The local inspector, Inspector Samaddar, is well known to me.

15 September

Who knew my strange and weird experience with Khoka would end like this? I got no chance at all in the last couple of days to write my diary. Only I can tell how much stress and anxiety I have had to suffer. The reason was simply that my fears turned out to be well founded. Avinash Babu did go around everywhere, talking about Khoka and describing the way he behaved. The same evening, curious visitors began making enquiries at my house.

Khoka was in his room on the first floor. At first, I tried to get rid of these unwelcome visitors by telling them that Khoka was asleep. But naturally, I could not pretend that he was sleeping all the time. At around eight o'clock, when my living room started to look decidedly crowded, and most people declared that they would not budge until they had seen Khoka, I was obliged to bring him down.

At once, everyone fell upon him, trying to get a close look. This time, I had to put my foot down. 'Look,' I said, as firmly as possible, 'he is only four years old. If you crowd around him like this, you'll cut off all the fresh air. He'll certainly fall ill if you don't let him breathe!'

At this, someone shouted, 'Well then, why don't you take him outside in the garden?'

This seemed a good idea. So I took him out. So far, Khoka had not stepped out of the house. As soon as he found himself in the garden, he began talking, rattling off the Latin name of every plant, bush, tree, leaf and flower he could see. Among the visitors was Father Galway, the headmaster of the local missionary school, who happened to be botanist. The extent of Khoka's knowledge of botany stupefied him. I saw him sink down in my wicker chair.

All this happened the day before yesterday. Last night, before going to bed, Khoka himself told me how many people had visited my house. According to him, the total number was 356, out of which three were Europeans, seven were from Orissa, five from Assam, one was a Japanese, fifty-six were Biharis, two were from Madras, and the rest were all Bengalis.

Yesterday morning, three reporters arrived from Calcutta, determined to speak to Khoka. Khoka obliged, but refused to answer any of their questions. All he told them—individually—was how much newsprint and ink their papers used, how many lines of news were printed in each issue, and the total number of papers printed.

One of the reporters was accompanied by a photographer. At one point, I saw him raise his camera and flash gun to take a picture. 'Don't use the flash,' Khoka told him, 'it will hurt my eyes.'

The photographer smiled. 'Just one photo, Khoka Babu,' he said, using a babyish tone, 'You'll look very nice in this photo, you'll see!'

He then proceeded to take a picture, but the flash refused to work. There was nothing wrong with the bulb, as it turned out. As many as seven bulbs were used, but the bright flash one expected each time just didn't appear.

In the evening, another gentleman arrived from Calcutta. His name was Sameeran Choudhury, he said. 'What can I do for you?' I asked.

It turned out that he was an impressario. That is to say, he arranged shows for gifted singers, musicians and dancers. He wanted Khoka to do a show of his own at the New Empire Theatre in Calcutta. He could answer questions from the audience, do complex mathematical sums, rattle off a few Latin names, sing and recite poetry. This would not just make him famous, but also give him an income. Depending on his success here, he could even be sent abroad one day.

'I cannot accept your proposal,' I said, 'without consulting Khoka's parents. All I can do is give you his father's name and address. You may go and see him.'

The evening wore on, and it soon became dark. Khoka was still facing an audience of nearly five hundred people and making astounding remarks. But, suddenly, he said in a low voice, '*Mir ist mude.*'

I happen to know several languages. German is one I am quite familiar with. I could understand Khoka's words. He was telling me in German, 'I am tired.' I did not waste another minute. The audience was told that Khoka was going to return to his room, he wanted to rest. People might have raised objections to his sudden departure, but the presence of a few policemen eased the situation.

I kept Khoka in my own room that night.

At around midnight, he seemed to be fast asleep. I put my book away and switched the light off. I was feeling quite depressed. I like peace and quiet. Handling large crowds in the last couple of days had made me tired too, although normally I don't get tired that easily. In the past, I have had to work through the night, for as many as four nights in a row on one occasion, and still not felt any fatigue at all. The truth was that I was worried about Khoka himself admitting to feeling tired.

What was going to happen to this extraordinary boy? I could take him back to his parents, but no one would leave him alone, would they? Curious spectators would start hounding him even in his own house. Besides, the whole point in bringing him here was to get to the bottom of the business. I could consult a specialist, but even that was not likely to help. Even before I had heard about Khoka's case, I had read quite a lot about brain diseases. Over the last few days, I had finished reading eleven books that spoke of nothing but possible abnormalities of the human brain. Nowhere did I find any mention of a similar case. There is no doubt that what has happened to Khoka is unique and hitherto unknown to man.

Turning these thoughts over in my mind, at some point I must have fallen asleep. What woke me was a clap of thunder. I opened my eyes to see lightning flash frequently, and heard a rumbling in the sky. The room suddenly lit up as there was another flash of lightning and, in that split second, I happened to glance at the other bed in my room. Khoka wasn't there.

I jumped to my feet. An odd instinct made me lift my pillow and look for the bunch of keys I'd kept there. The whole bunch was gone. Without losing another moment, I ran down the stairs and went straight to my laboratory. Its door was thrown wide open, and a light had been switched on.

I stepped in. What I saw froze my blood.

Khoka was sitting on a high stool, facing my work table. In front of him, laid out in rows, were bottles of poisonous and lethal acids. The Bunsen burner had been lit, and in a flask, placed next to it, was a liquid of some kind. It appeared to have been heated in the last few minutes. Khoka was clutching the bottle that contained Terrinium Phosphate.

He tilted the bottle and poured just a few drops into the flask. At once, coils of yellow smoke began rising from the mixture, filling the room with a sharp, pungent smell. My eyes started smarting.

Khoka realized I was in the room. He turned his head to look at me. 'Where's the Annihilin?' he barked.

Annihilin? Khoka wanted my Annihilin? It was the most potent acid of all. I kept it on the top shelf of a cupboard, and that cupboard remained locked most of the time. But then, the bottles that Khoka had already managed to get hold of contained enough material to destroy at least thirty elephants.

'Get me the Annihilin!' he commanded, 'Now. I need it.'

I tried to control my emotions. 'Khoka,' I said, slowly walking towards the boy, 'All these things that you're handling are quite harmful. If a single drop falls on your hand, it will burn your skin, you'll feel a lot of pain. Let's go back upstairs, to our room. Come on!'

I stretched a hand towards him. Khoka responded by suddenly picking up the bottle of Terrinium Phosphate and raising it over his head, as if he would throw it at me if I took another step forward. If he did that, I knew I would be permanently crippled, even if I didn't die.

This time, Khoka spoke through clenched teeth, the bottle still aimed at me. 'Give me that Annihilin—if you know what's good for you!'

There was nothing that I could do to get out of the situation. But what gave me a degree of reassurance was the fact that Khoka had already handled quite a few acids, without hurting himself. So I unlocked the cupboard and picked up the bottle of Annihilin from the back of the top shelf. Then I placed it in front of Khoka, and began praying silently.

To my surprise, Khoka lifted the stopper and, very carefully, poured only three drops of Annihilin into the flask. Then, before I could say or do anything, Khoka picked up the flask and drank the green mixture in it that he had prepared himself, finishing it in four quick gulps. In the next instant, his body went limp and he fell over the desk.

I ran across, picked him up in my arms and ran all the way back to my bedroom. Having put him back in his bed, I quickly felt his pulse. It appeared to be normal. He was breathing naturally, and his face looked calm. He did not seem to have lost consciousness. On the contrary, he appeared simply asleep, sunk into a deep, natural slumber.

Outside, the heavens had opened in a torrential downpour. I sat quietly by Khoka's bed. About an hour later, the rain gradually stopped and the clouds dispersed. Dawn was just breaking. Crows and sparrows started their morning chorus.

Exactly at five minutes past six, Khoka stirred, turned on his side and opened his eyes. The look in his eyes was different. He seemed a little lost and uncertain. He looked around the room, then spoke, sounding as if he was about to cry. 'Where's Mummy?' he asked. 'I want my Mummy!'

*

I took Khoka back to his parents and returned home only an hour ago. He and I quickly became friends on our way to Jhajha. When I left his house, Khoka stood at the door, waved at me and said, 'Will you bring me sweets, Dadu? Toffees?'

'Of course,' I replied, 'I will come back from Giridih tomorrow, and I will certainly bring you sweets!'

To myself, I said silently, 'Even a day ago, Khoka Babu, you would not have asked me for sweets and toffees. What you might have demanded would have been some peculiar object with a complex, unpronouncable Latin name!'

Translated by Gopa Majumdar

PROFESSOR SHONKU AND THE SPOOK

10 April

I have believed, for a long time, that one day things such as ghosts and spectres, seances, telepathy and clairvoyance will become subjects for scientific study. I have heard, many a time, first-hand accounts of encounters with ghosts, from people who are sensible and trustworthy, and not given to irrational flights of fancy. So I have not been able to dismiss the concept of ghosts, or life after death, as complete nonsense.

Mind you, I have never had such an experience myself. A Chinese magician was once successful in hypnotizing me; I have, on one occasion, had to struggle with an invisible adversary, and seen a sadhu turn a heap of bones into a living, breathing creature. But I have never come face to face with the ghost of a dead man.

It was possibly for this reason that, of late, the desire to see a ghost was getting stronger in my mind. I kept wondering if there might be a scientific way to make an apparition present itself.

Naturally, in this case, chemicals and scientific instruments alone could not achieve anything. What was required was concentration. I had to have that—as much as I could muster—for there would be no point in being able to see any ordinary ghost. I wanted to call the departed souls of specific people to my room, talk to them, and then send them back to the other world. If I could bring them as real people who could be felt and touched, if I could shake hands with them, that would be my biggest achievement. An achievement for science!

As a result of my hard work over the last three months, all my careful research and craftsmanship, my new machine called Neo-spectroscope is now ready. The term 'spectro' is related to 'spectre' here, not 'spectrum'. And it is 'neo', for no one has ever built such a machine before.

A detailed description of this machine is already given in my main notebook. There is no need to repeat that here in my diary. Briefly, what I did is this: I built a metal helmet to fit my head. Two electric wires come out of this helmet, which go into a glass bowl filled with a solution that I have made. Soaking in that solution are two flat pieces of copper. The two wires are connected to the copper. At one glance, my contraption might remind people of an acid battery.

A variety of ingredients have gone into making the

solution. The most important of these is the juice from the roots of some trees in our cremation ground, which have been nourished by the smoke from several funeral pyres, over many years.

When this solution is heated over a gas burner, thick coils of green smoke rise from it, forming a column that shoots up to a height of five and a half feet. Rather extraordinarily, it does not spread anywhere, but remains hovering over the glass bowl. It is through this column of smoke that a ghost is supposed to appear.

This morning, I tested my machine for the first time. I cannot say I was entirely successful, chiefly because I failed to concentrate fully. Just as I was going into my laboratory, I saw Newton pounce upon a cockroach in one corner of the veranda, and kill it with his paw. As a result, when I put the helmet on and began to think of a suitable ghost, all I could think of was the lifeless form of the cockroach.

Possibly for this reason, five minutes later, I could clearly see a huge cockroach taking shape in the column of smoke, waving its antennae at me. This spectre of the cockroach remained visible for nearly a minute. Then it disappeared. Obviously, it was useless to try for a proper ghost after that.

I shall try again tomorrow morning. Today, I must spend as much time as I can in practising mental exercises. I must not lose my concentration tomorrow.

11 April

Unbelievable.

This morning, I had a conversation for almost three and a half minutes with my dear, departed friend,

Archibald Ackroyd, the British scientist. He died in Norway under suspicious circumstances.Today, incredibly, the same Ackroyd appeared amidst the coils of green smoke in my lab.

I had been thinking of him most intently for five minutes, when the first thing that became visible through the smoke was a human skeleton. Its right hand was stretched towards me.

Then, suddenly, a pair of glasses appeared on the skeleton's face—bifocal glasses with a golden frame. I had no difficulty in recognizing them. They belonged to Ackroyd.

After the glasses appeared a pipe, hanging out of the skeleton's mouth, its teeth clenched round its handle. The pipe was Ackroyd's favourite briar.

Then I saw a watch and chain, just below the ribcage. They too, were well known to me.

Obviously, those objects on Ackroyd's person that had made an impression on my mind, were the first to appear.

Suddenly, the skeleton spoke. 'Hello, Shonku.'

It was Ackroyd's voice, and no mistake. Almost at once, the skeleton disappeared and, in its place, the full form of Ackroyd's body appeared: tall, handsome, clad in a suit, mackintosh and gloves. His lips were parted in the same sweet, childlike smile that I knew so well. A lock of his salt-and-pepper hair had fallen on his forehead.

I stretched out my own hand and was about to shake Ackroyd's, when I remembered that what I could see was not the real man, but only his shape, his likeness; and it was hanging in mid-air. Slightly

embarrassed, I withdrew my hand. The strange thing was that his voice was amazingly clear. Before I could say anything, he spoke again in that deep yet melodious voice.

'I have been watching your work. I like to keep track of all your achievements. Your country should be proud of you.'

Excitement had made my throat go dry. But I managed to speak. 'What do you think of my Neo-spectroscope?'

Ackroyd smiled through the hazy green smoke. 'You can see me, can't you? You don't really need my views. You've been successful, and you know it. Views of others are immaterial to those who have left your world. In ours, emotions and feelings have no meaning. Worries, anxieties, grief or joy—everything is irrelevant.'

I heard these words in silence, still feeling profoundly amazed, and was just thinking what to ask him next, when Ackroyd gave a funny smile and was gone, as if he were a bubble that had suddenly burst. Then the heavy coils of smoke seemed to be moving, getting closer to me . . . and I could feel my consciousness slipping away.

When I came to, Prahlad was splashing water on my face. 'Why are you wearing an iron hat in this heat, babu? You shouldn't be doing this at your age!' he told me.

I took off my helmet. I felt exhausted, which was clearly the result of working my brain too hard. But there could be no doubt that the spirit of my friend, Ackroyd, visited my laboratory and exchanged a few words with me. All my research, all my hard work has been successful to a large extent. My Neo-spectroscope is a truly astounding discovery.

Well, I must not let physical fatigue discourage me. Tomorrow, I intend to sit once more with my machine. What I'd like to do is meet one or two characters from history, and have a direct conversation.

12 April

Today, I had meant to get Siraj-ud-daula in my laboratory to find out the truth behind the episode of the black hole in Calcutta. But my neighbour, Avinash Chatterjee, arrived and ruined all my plans.

I had just finished my coffee in the living room and was wiping my mouth with a napkin, when he turned up. I doubt if there is another person in the whole world with such a totally unscientific attitude as Avinash Babu. The fellow should have been born in the Stone Age. He is a misfit in the twentieth century. All I have ever seen him do is express complete indifference to my successes as a scientist, and mock me over my failures.

He entered the room and promptly sat down on a sofa. 'Why were you loitering near the Usri?' he asked.

Usri is the name of our river. It is true that I go there sometimes on my morning walks, but over the last twenty days or so, I haven't been there. As a matter of fact, I haven't set foot outside my house at all.

So I said, 'When did you see me loitering?'

'Today. Only about an hour ago. I called out to you, but you didn't reply.'

'What! How is that possible? I did not leave the house this morning, even once.'

Avinash Babu burst out laughing. 'What's the matter with you? Why are you denying your movements? If you keep doing this, people will get decidedly suspicious. The man I saw was about five feet two inches tall like you, had a beard exactly like yours, and was bald, just like you. How many men in Giridih fit that description?'

A mixture of wonder and annoyance rendered me

speechless. What did Avinash Babu take me for? A liar? Me, Trilokeshwar Shonku? Admittedly, in the past I have sometimes had to hide my valuable formulae from other scientists who have shown an excessive interest in my work; but if I did go to the riverside this morning, why should I try to hide that simple fact from someone as insignificant as Avinash Babu?

'And it wasn't just I who saw you,' Avinash Babu went on, 'Ramlochan Banerjee saw you, too. But it was not by the river. He found you in the mango grove behind our judge's house. That was *after* I saw you. He just told me, on my way here. You can ask him, if you like.'

I remained silent. Not only was Avinash Babu lying himself, but he was also suggesting that Banerjee—an old and respected man—was doing the same. I could not fathom why Avinash Babu should do such a thing.

Prahlad appeared with a cup of coffee. Avinash Babu suddenly asked him a question: 'Prahlad,' he said, 'was your babu at home all morning, or did he go out?'

'Last night he was pottering in the lab until quite late,' Prahlad replied, 'So how could he go out early this morning? No, he was at home.'

I must mention something here. I did not go to my laboratory after yesterday morning. I never go there without a reason. All I did yesterday, after my encounter with Ackroyd, was practise concentration. But I did that in my bedroom. At nine last night, I went to bed and rose this morning, as always, at five. How could Prahlad say that I was pottering in the lab late last night?

'When I was working in the lab,' I asked Prahlad, 'did you bring me coffee at any time?'

'Of course. You were fiddling with your things in

the dark, so I . . .'

'In the dark?' I interrupted him, 'If it was dark, how can you be so sure that it was me, and not someone else?'

Prahlad grinned. 'How could I not recognize you, babu? There was so much moonlight. It fell on your bald head, and it was shining like . . .'

'All right, all right.'

Avinash Babu lit a beedi. 'Once I saw a film,' he told me, 'It had a funny story. There was this man, who got split in two. So, at any given time, you could see one half in one place, and the other somewhere else. Do you think a similar thing has happened to you? I shouldn't be surprised. How many times have I told you not to do these weird experiments? One's brain gets affected by such things. But would you listen? Oh no!'

He spent another half an hour in my house, chiefly leafing through a magazine. As he turned its pages, I caught him casting sidelong glances at me. I could say nothing to him, for my mind was in complete turmoil.

In the evening, I walked over to Ramlochan Banerjee's house. He was sitting on his front veranda, chatting with the local doctor. When he saw me arrive, he said, 'You should start using a hearing aid. I called out to you this morning so many times. But you didn't seem to hear me at all. What were you doing in that mango grove, anyway? What were you looking for? A plant of some kind?'

I smiled a little foolishly, and offered an imaginary explanation for my supposed preoccupation this morning. Then I said goodbye and made my way to the river. Was I really going mad? Such a thing had never happened before. I have spent the last twenty-seven years in Giridih. A large chunk of that time has been spent in doing difficult and complex research work. But never before has anyone told me that my normal behaviour has changed because of all that work. So what was wrong today?

After dinner, I couldn't help going into the laboratory once more. The Neo-spectroscope was lying exactly where I'd left it. My notebooks, papers and all the apparatus were all in their places.

Did I come here last night? If I did, how could I have forgotten all about it? It was impossible.

I switched the light off. Moonlight came streaming through the southern window and fell on the table. I walked towards the window, my mind full of anxious thoughts.

I could see my garden from here. I sat in that garden every evening, on my favourite deck chair, under a colourful umbrella. That umbrella was still there, as was the chair. It should have been empty. But I could see someone sitting in it.

There was no one in my house except Prahlad and Newton. Prahlad would never sit in my chair, unless he went totally insane.

The man sitting there was old. He was bald, except for a little hair around his ears. He had an unkempt beard and moustache. Although I could only see his profile and he did not turn his face toward me even once, it was clear that there were startling resemblances between his appearance and my own.

I wonder if anyone else has ever had a similar

experience. If a man has a twin, he may get used to seeing himself in his brother. But I don't have a brother at all, let alone a twin. The only male cousin I have lives in Bareilly, and his height is 6'2". Who was this man in my garden?

Suddenly I had an idea. Could it be that some youngster had put on a disguise to look like me and was simply playing a practical joke? That must be it. What else could it be? There was a theatre group in Baraganda. One of them must be responsible for this prank.

I decided to catch him red-handed. So I stole out silently, crossed the passage outside and reached the garden.

But it was in vain. When I got to the chair, it was empty. I touched the canvas and found it warm. It could only mean that someone was sitting there just a few moments ago. I looked around quickly. There was no one. In that bright moonlight, everything was clearly visible. Except for the golancha tree, there was nowhere that a man could hide.

Had my own eyes played tricks? But then, who had Avinash Babu and Mr Banerjee seen? Who was he?

I returned to my bedroom, feeling more agitated than ever. If I don't take a pill, I will not be able to sleep tonight.

14 April

The manner in which the mystery of the double Shonku was solved, is something that no other experience in my entire life can match.

Over the last two days, I did not step out of my

bedroom for fear of running into the second 'me'. I told Prahlad to lock the door of my bedroom from outside and place a large, heavy table against it, to stop myself from leaving the room by mistake. Prahlad did as he was told, and brought my meals, as well as cups of coffee, directly to my bedroom. Each time, he had to remove the table and unlock the door. He waited in the room until I finished eating, then took the used plates and cups away, locking the door behind him and replacing the table.

In spite of these measures, each day Prahlad received news of people having seen 'me' in various places in Giridih, but chiefly by the river. Everyone who had seen me, was convinced that I had gone completely crazy, which was the reason why I was not responding to their greetings. Last evening, Prahlad said, the doctor had come to my house quite voluntarily to examine me. But Prahlad told him I was asleep.

This morning, I could not bear it any more. So I called Prahlad and had him unlock the door. Then I went straight to my laboratory.

My chair, my table, the new machine, the electric wires, the container for the solution—everything was where it should be. The empty chair seemed inviting. I went and sat in it. Then I poured some of the solution into a beaker and lit a burner. When I placed the beaker over the burner, green smoke began to rise from it almost at once.

Then I wore the helmet, and made sure that the wires remained in contact with the copper plates placed in the beaker.

My eyes remained fixed on the spiralling smoke. In

my mind was a picture of the unfortunate Nawab of Bengal in the eighteenth century, Nawab Siraj-ud-daula. All other thought was excluded.

Slowly, a skeleton appeared in the column of smoke. As soon as its hazy outlines became clear, it was obvious that only the top half had appeared. There was the skull, the neck and the ribcage, but nothing else.

How very strange! How did this happen?

A few moments later a turban, embroidered with gold thread, appeared on the skull. This was followed by two glittering diamond studs on its earlobes.

It came to me in a flash. All the pictures of Siraj-ud-daula that I had seen in history books showed his face and torso. That was the picture I had in mind and so only those portions of his body, as seen in the picture, had now appeared before my eyes.

I was still staring at the skeleton and had just noticed the pupil in one of the eyes being formed, when a sudden guffaw broke my concentration. In the next instant, the upper half of Siraj-ud-daula's body vanished.

Then, purely unexpectedly, a figure emerged from the green smoke, stepped out of it and walked towards my table. Who was this? Was it my own reflection in a mirror? Or was it someone else? I had no idea that two different men could look so much like carbon copies of each other.

The stranger spoke. The sound of his voice told me at once that it was no reflection. He cast an unnaturally sharp glance in my direction and said, 'Trilokeshwar, I am grateful to you. You have helped me fulfil a long-cherished dream.'

I swallowed and somehow managed to find my voice. 'Who are you?' I asked.

'I will tell you, have patience. Once upon a time, I used to sit by the Usri for my meditation. I left home when I was sixteen and became a follower of Golok Baba. He was a tantric sadhu. One day, a vicious hailstorm started while I was sitting outside, lost in my meditation. A hailstone fell on my head with such force that it killed me.'

'Killed . . . ?'

'Yes. Ever since that day, I have often wanted to return here. But it wasn't possible for me to assume a finite shape and do what I wanted to do. Your scientific skills and my own knowledge of tantra have now made that possible. I was here on the very first day when you were sitting in that chair. But I did not let you see me, as I had some other work to finish first. You see, my sudden death meant that some of the tools and other material I used for my tantric practices were left behind. I did not get the chance to dispose of them. Yet I knew if they fell into the wrong hands, they might cause a great deal of harm. So, having spent the last few days looking for them, I finally found those objects today and threw them into the river. There is no cause for concern any more.'

'But . . . but . . . I need to know who you are!'

'Yes, I am coming to that. There is something else you need to know. You have been thinking of only those souls who are incapable for assuming a finite form. None of them has the special powers my tantric meditations have given me. Besides, none of them has ties of blood with you.'

'Ties of blood? Do I have . . . are you . . . ?'

'Yes. I am your great-great-great-grandfather, the late Botukeshwar Shonku. Born in 1730, died in 1807. Come, let us shake hands.'

My ancestor, whose appearance was totally identical to mine, offered me his hand. As soon as I touched it, I felt a tremor run through my body. Botukeshwar's hand was freezing cold. He laughed. 'Does that feel cold? All right, I'd better go.'

He dropped my hand and sprang back into the smoky column. In just a few seconds, his body was reduced to a skeleton. Before that skeleton disappeared from view, it bent its head and showed me a little hole in its crown.

*

Having met a ghost in the flesh, I no longer felt any interest in meeting an intangible form. So I put my Neo-spectroscope away. To tell the truth, the mental strain the whole thing was causing me, was getting too much.

I was playing with Newton in the living room a little later, when Avinash Babu turned up. He looked both worried and agitated. Having taken a seat, for a whole minute he remained silent. All he did was stare at the floor and frown. Then he spoke: 'You know my nephew, Shibu, don't you?'

'Yes.'

'He . . . well, he likes taking photos. So, when he heard that you were denying being seen outside your house even though various people had seen you here and there, Shibu decided to . . . to play a prank. He took his camera to the riverside and hid behind a tree, until he saw you arrive. Then he quickly took your picture.'

'Good. Have you brought it with you?'

'No. There was no point in bringing it. All that the picture shows is the river, the sandy bank and rocks. Shibu saw you standing quite close to those rocks. You should have been in the picture, but you're not. You've vanished!'

I smiled. 'Shall I tell you who it was?' I remarked, 'It wasn't me, but the ghost of one of my ancestors. Come on now, have a cup of coffee. Prahlad!'

Translated by Gopa Majumdar

Professor Shonku and Robu

16 April

Today I received a reply from the famous German scientist, Professor Paumer. This is what he wrote:

> Dear Professor Shonku
>
> I was very pleased to receive your letter, and read your description of the robot that you have built. But your account caused me more wonder than anything else. You say that you have read my articles related to my research on robots, and that you have learnt a lot from them. However, it must be said that if your robot really fits your description, then you have far exceeded my own achievements.
>
> I am too old to travel all the way to India.

But if you can bring your robot here, not only will I be pleased but it will also help me in my own work. There is another scientist in Heidelberg—Dr Borgelt. He, too, has been working on building robots. Perhaps I could introduce you to him.

If you agree to come, I can arrange to pay for your travel at least one-way. Needless to say, you will stay with me as my guest.

I wait to hear from you.

Yours sincerely
Rudolph Paumer

I have already replied to Paumer, telling him to expect me around the middle of next month. I accepted his offer of financial help as travelling to Germany will be an expensive business, though I have often wished to see the country.

My Robu will naturally go with me. In the coming weeks, I am going to teach him to speak German. Right now, he can only manage English and Bengali. If he can learn German, Paumer can talk to him directly, without having to rely on me to act as an interpreter.

It took me a year and a half to build Robu. I built him from scratch, though Prahlad assisted me at times by handing me the tools I needed. The most amazing thing about the whole exercise was the small amount of money within which I managed. The total sum came to Rs 333.85. The final product, built with this tiny sum, will act as my right-hand man in the laboratory. Robu takes less than a second to do simple additions,

subtractions, multiplication and divisions. I don't think he'd take more than ten seconds to solve any complex mathematical problem. That just goes to show what an absolute gem I've found—for a song. I say 'found' because I cannot see any scientific invention as purely man-made. The possibility—or potential—of any invention or discovery must pre-exist. All man can do, is either use his brain to work out this possibility, or find it through pure chance, and put it to his own use.

I cannot say that Robu's appearance is attractive. His eyes look as if he has a squint. In order to override the squint, I have given him a smile. No matter how difficult or complex the problem he's told to solve, his mouth is always spread in a slight smile. But he cannot move his lips as he speaks. If I were to add an extra mechanism to make his lips move, it would have cost me more money and extra time. So he only has a little hole between his lips, through which he can speak.

Inside his head—where normal people have a brain—Robu has a number of electric wires, batteries and valves. It cannot, therefore, do many of the functions that a human brain does. For instance, Robu does not have emotions. He cannot feel joy, grief, or even anger and envy. All he can do is answer questions and carry out tasks. He can handle mathematical questions of all kinds, but cannot answer any other question unless he has been taught the answer. I have taught him 50,000 questions and answers in Bengali and English. Not once has he made a mistake when I have put him to the test. Now, if I teach him answers to around 10,000 questions in German, we shall be ready to depart for Germany.

Robu may not be perfect, but I don't think any other robot in the world can do as much as he can. But there is no point in keeping him in a small place like Giridih. Shouldn't the world learn how much a scientist in India has been able to accomplish, working with limited resources, and on a very small budget? If the word spreads, it will mean more glory for my country than myself. At any rate, that is what I am aiming for.

18 April

Today, at last, Avinash Babu acknowledged my scientific skills. Avinash Babu is my neighbour. On the whole, he is a good man, but sometimes I find it difficult to put up with his habit of making fun of my research and experiments.

In the last three months, every time he turned up for a chat, I got Prahlad to tell him that I was too busy to see anyone. Today, he arrived just as I had finished the final German lesson for Robu, and was sitting in my laboratory, turning the pages of a journal. I told Prahlad to bring him straight to the lab, since I wanted him to meet Robu.

Avinash Babu walked in, screwed up his nose and said, 'Have you been using heeng?' Then his eyes fell on Robu and promptly grew round. 'Oh my God! What is that? A radio? A gramophone? Or what?'

In reply, I said, 'Ask him. He'll tell you. His name is Robu.'

'A robuscope?'

'No, no. Why are you adding "scope" to his name? He's simply called Robu. Go on, ask him what he is, he'll tell you.'

'Is this a new game?' asked Avinash Babu and turned to face Robu. 'All right then, dear Robu, what are you?'

Robu's reply came clearly through the little hole in his mouth. 'I am a mechanical man. Professor Shonku's assistant.'

Avinash Babu nearly collapsed in amazement. Then

he heard a list of everything that Robu had learnt to do, and even saw a few examples. His face turned pale. All Avinash Babu could do after that, was grab my hands and shake them vigorously. Then he left. That told me that this time, he was truly impressed.

Later, I found an article by Professor Borgelt in an old German magazine. It was on robots. He had said, rather arrogantly, that the skill that scientists in Germany had shown in building robots could not be matched by any other country. He also appeared to think that while a robot could learn to obey commands and work like a slave, it could never learn to use its brain independently.

The article included a photograph. Borgelt's forehead was broad, his eyebrows extraordinarily thick, eyes sunken and, in the middle of his chin, was a square goatee.

Having read his article and seen his photo, now I feel a strong desire to meet him.

23 May

I reached Heidelberg this morning. The place is as pretty as a picture. Europe's oldest university is situated in Heidelberg. The river Neckar flows through the city, and behind it, standing guard, is a mountain covered by a green forest. On top of this mountain is Heidelberg's historic castle.

Paumer's house is five miles from the main city, amidst most picturesque surroundings. I haven't got words to describe the warmth and cordiality with which the seventy-year-old scientist received me. 'You must know of the ties between Germany and India,' he said. 'I have read some of your ancient literature and philosophy. Max Mueller translated those most beautifully. We are all much indebted to him. What you have accomplished as an Indian scientist, is a matter of pride not just for your own country, but Germany as well!'

Robu was lying in his case, packed tightly and carefully with cotton wool, straw and sawdust. I knew Paumer was very curious to see him; so I brought him out, wiped him clean and put him on his feet in a corner of Paumer's laboratory. In spite of all his research on robots and his articles, Paumer had never built one himself.

He did nothing to hide his surprise on seeing my Robu. 'Why, you seem to have put him together simply with glue and nails and sticking plaster! You mean this robot can speak and do things?' Paumer sounded openly sceptical.

I smiled. 'You can test him if you like. Ask him a question.'

Paumer turned to Robu. '*Welche arbeit machst du?*' (What kind of work do you do?)

Robu replied clearly and distinctly, '*Ich hilfe meinem herrn bei seiner arbeit, und lose mathematische probleme.*' (I help my master in his work, and solve mathematical problems.)

Paumer stared at Robu for a few moments, then nodded his head slowly. 'Shonku,' he said with a sigh, 'I cannot think of any equivalent in the history of science that can match what you have done. Borgelt may well feel envious.'

We had so far, not spoken of Borgelt. The sudden mention of his name startled me somewhat. Had Borgelt built a robot, too?

But before I could ask anything, Paumer continued to speak. 'Borgelt lives in Heidelberg—in a remote spot, like me. It's on the other side of the river. I knew him well. Once we were close enough to be seen as friends. We went to the same school in Berlin, though I was senior to him by three years. Then I came to Heidelberg for further studies, and he remained in Berlin. He came here about ten years ago, to live in his old ancestral home.'

'Has he built a robot himself?' I couldn't help asking.

'He's been trying to do that, for quite some time. But I don't think he's had any luck. In fact, I heard that he had a nervous breakdown. He hasn't been seen outside his house in the last six months. A few times, I tried to speak to him on the phone; but each time I rang, his butler said that Borgelt was unwell. I haven't called him recently.'

'Does he know I am here?'

'I don't know. I did tell a few other scientists about your visit. You'll soon get to meet them. Some press reporters might have heard—but no, I saw no reason to inform Borgelt separately.'

I said nothing more. A cuckoo clock on the wall announced that it was four o'clock. I could see a portion of the garden through the open window. In the distance was a hill. There was no noise except the chirping of birds.

Paumer said, 'Stregonoff of Russia, Steinway of America and Dr Mannings of England . . . they have all built robots. Three or four robots have been produced in Germany. I have seen all of them. I can tell you that none of them was built so simply, or is capable of such clear speech.'

'My Robu can do calculations, too. Give him any mathematical problem, and he'll solve it for you.'

'Really? You mean he would know something like Auerbach's equation?'

'Ask him.'

Paumer turned to Robu again and asked some questions. Robu's answers astounded him. 'My word, it's like magic!' he exclaimed. 'Congratulations once more.' Then he fell silent. A few minutes later, Paumer suddenly asked, 'Can your Robu feel emotion, like humans?'

'No. That's one thing he cannot do.'

'Pity. It would have been really good if there was some sort of link between your own brain and his. If he could share your joy and grief, then he would really be a useful, reliable companion for you.'

Paumer seemed to grow a little preoccupied. After a pause, he continued, 'I have thought a great deal about this. I mean, about how to make mechanical man understand a human's feelings. I did a lot of work and made considerable progress, you know. But then I became old and ill. My heart began to give me trouble. So I could not build my own robot, as I had meant to do, and carry out experiments on it.'

I replied, 'I am perfectly happy with the work that my Robu does for me. I do not want anything more.'

Paumer said nothing. He was looking steadily at Robu. Robu was standing still, the same smile on his lips. The afternoon sun fell on his left eye, and made it glitter. It seemed as if his eye, made with an electric bulb, was also smiling.

24 May

It is now midnight. I am sitting in my room on the first floor of Paumer's house. I must try to describe, as coherently as I can, everything that's happened since midnight yesterday. How far I'll succeed, I do not know because I am feeling greatly disturbed. For the first time in my life, I am beginning to wonder if I am really the gifted scientist that I always thought I was. If what I thought was correct, then why did I have to face such embarrassment today?

I should first explain what happened last night. It was only a minor incident, but worth recording.

Paumer and I finished our dinner at nine. Then we spent a long time chatting over coffee, which we had in his living room. I noticed that Paumer was growing preoccupied again from time to time. I couldn't tell what he was thinking. Perhaps Robu had reminded him of his own inability to work as he used to. It is true that Paumer looks old and infirm. It seems highly unlikely that he will ever be able to do any new research on robots.

I said good-night to Paumer and went to bed a little after ten. Before retiring upstairs, we looked in on Robu. He seemed happy enough in Paumer's laboratory. The weather in Germany, or its natural splendour, was of no importance to Robu. He seemed to be waiting only for an instruction from me. Both Paumer and I wished him good-night in German. Robu's reply came at once, also in German: *'Gute nacht, Herr Professor Shonku. Gute nacht, Herr Professor Paumer!'*

After getting into bed, I spent some time leafing through a journal. Then, when I heard the grandfather clock under the stairs strike eleven, I switched off my bedside lamp and fell asleep.

I do not know what time it was, when I suddenly woke in the middle of the night. It was a noise that had woken me, and it was coming from Paumer's laboratory, which was right below my bedroom. Tap, tap, tap, clang, clang, tap, tap! At times, it sounded like footsteps on a wooden floor, at others it was as if someone was lifting machinery.

The noises stopped in about five minutes. Even so, I remained awake for some time, straining my ears. But I heard nothing, except the clock striking three.

In the morning, I met Paumer at breakfast, but chose to say nothing about the strange noises. Had I done so, Paumer might have been embarrassed and thought that I was complaining because my sleep had been disturbed.

After breakfast, I wanted to go out for a walk, but before we could leave the table, Paumer's servant, Kurt, arrived with a visiting card in his hand and passed it to his master. Paumer glanced at it and looked surprised. 'Why, Borgelt is here!' he exclaimed.

I felt considerably taken aback by this news.

Paumer and I made our way to the living room. One glance at the man seated on a sofa showed me the same face I had seen in that magazine; but his hair seemed to have gone far more grey. Borgelt rose upon seeing us, and offered us his greetings. He too, must have been close to seventy, but I found his manner surprisingly brisk.

'Why, Borgelt,' said Paumer, 'you certainly do not

look as if you've been ailing for a long time. On the contrary, I'd say that you looked as if you'd been on holiday and come back much refreshed!'

Borgelt laughed. His voice was deep. 'I tell people I'm unwell only to be left alone. If I say I'm busy, no one pays the slightest attention. If anything, they become more curious than ever and start ringing me frequently to ask why I'm so busy. I can hardly tell everyone the real reason, every time they ask.'

'That is very true,' Paumer agreed. Then he offered Borgelt a drink. Borgelt shook his head. 'No, thank you. I've given up drinking. Besides, I haven't got a lot of time today. This morning I read a press report about Professor Shonku's visit and saw a picture of his robot. You know about my interest in this matter. So I came without calling you first. I hope you don't mind?'

'No, not in the least.'

'Perhaps you'd like to look at my robot?' I asked.

'Yes, that's why I am here. I am naturally curious to see how you were able to accomplish what appeared totally impossible.'

We took Borgelt to the laboratory. The first thing Borgelt said upon seeing Robu was, 'You did not pay much attention to its appearance, did you? I think it would be better to call it simply a machine, rather than a mechanical man.'

I could hardly argue with this. 'Yes,' I admitted, 'I paid more attention to his performance than his looks. No one can say he's as handsome as Apollo!'

'I believe this robot is good at mathematics?'

'Do you want to test him?'

Borgelt looked at Robu. 'How much do two and

two make?'

The answer came instantly, but so loudly that the glass instruments in Paumer's lab shook and clattered for a while. It was most unusual for Robu to speak so loudly. I realized, with some surprise, that Borgelt's question had irritated Robu.

Robu's abrupt manner seemed to make Borgelt grow a little wary. He began asking further questions, each more complex than the other. Robu answered all of them correctly, and within seven seconds. My heart came close to bursting with pride. I could see beads of perspiration break out on Borgelt's forehead.

Five minutes later, he turned to me. 'What else does he know apart from mathematics?'

'He knows a lot about you. Ask him, if you like.'

Before we left Giridih, I had collected some information about Borgelt from a scientific *Who's Who* and fed it into Robu. I had anticipated that, if we met Borgelt, he would want to ask questions about himself.

But he seemed surprised by my revelation. 'Really? Your machine knows so much? All right, Herr Robu, what is my name?'

Robu remained silent. One second, two seconds, ten seconds, a whole minute passed . . . there was no reply, no sound, nothing. Robu appeared no different from the furniture in the room—still, lifeless, silent.

This time, it was my turn to break into a cold sweat. I went over to Robu, pressed a button on his head, fiddled with some of the other fittings, then shook him violently, more than once, to no avail. All the machinery fitted inside his body jingled and clanged, but Robu did not speak.

It wasn't just my own pride and self-esteem that lay in smithereens in the presence of two well-known German scientists. It was the prestige of Indian science that was at stake.

Borgelt snorted. 'Well, obviously there is some big defect,' he said. 'Anyway, at least he knows good maths. If you are not doing anything else tomorrow evening, you might consider bringing your robot over to my house. I may be able to fix whatever's gone wrong. Besides, I have something to show you. You are both invited.'

Borgelt left. Paumer, I could see, had understood my feelings and was feeling embarrassed himself. He said, 'I find this business most extraordinary. Come on, let's see if he can now answer questions.'

We turned back to Robu and began again. Robu answered—quite correctly—every question we asked. He moved and walked when asked to, without any difficulty. Clearly, some problem somewhere had cropped up only temporarily when Borgelt asked his own name. Robu could hardly be blamed for it. If it was anyone's fault, it was mine.

Borgelt rang us late in the evening to remind us of his invitation. He made it a point to include Robu in the invitation, and finished by saying, 'There will be no one here but myself. If your machine lets you down again, you needn't worry.'

However, I continued to feel uncomfortable. Afraid that so much anxiety might keep me awake at night, I took one of my own somnolin pills.

One thing keeps coming back to me. Why did I hear funny noises in the middle of the night yesterday? Was Paumer working in the laboratory? Did *he* fiddle with the machinery fitted inside Robu?

Had Paumer and Borgelt conspired together?

27 May

I will return to India tomorrow. I don't think I can ever forget my horrific experience in Heidelberg.

But I have learnt something new. I have realized that while a scientist may be worthy of one's respect, he need not necessarily be worthy of one's trust. Yet, when the whole thing happened, this was not what I was thinking. All that I could think of, was that I still had an awful lot of unfinished work. There was so little that I had finished doing. How was I going to save myself?

Perhaps I should explain fully what happened.

Paumer and I both felt we had to accept Borgelt's invitation. It is not easy to travel with Robu, but even so, I decided to take him with me since Borgelt had been so insistent. Around six that evening, a horse-drawn carriage turned up to take us to Borgelt's house. I packed Robu in his case and laid him down on a seat. Then I tied the case to the seat with a length of rope. Paumer and I sat on the seat opposite. Borgelt's house was about three miles from Paumer's, which meant that we would have to travel for forty-five minutes to get there.

I spent much of that time looking at the beautiful blossom on the trees that lined the streets, and listening to Paumer's account of Borgelt's ancestors. One of them—called Julius Borgelt—was a bit like Baron Frankenstein. Apparently he tried to bring a corpse back to life, and then died himself under mysterious circumstances. There were one or two others who were said to be insane, and spent most of their lives in asylums.

We entered a wood and made our journey through it going uphill. It felt appreciably cooler here. I wrapped my scarf tightly round my neck.

A little later, we went round a bend and came upon a huge, carved gate. Paumer said, 'Here we are!' Over the gate, written in ornate letters, were the words: Villa Marianne.

A guard opened the gate. Our carriage passed through and drove right up to the front door. It was really much more than an ordinary house. It would be better to call it a palace, or even a castle.

Borgelt was waiting for us. He shook our hands as we alighted, and said, 'I am very pleased you could come.' His hand felt cold.

Two tall and hefty servants came out and carried Robu's case inside. We were shown into the living room. Robu was taken to the adjoining library, brought out of his case and made to stand upright.

Everything in the house, particularly objects in the living room—pictures, mirrors, clocks and a chandelier—bore the stamp of not just antiquity but also class and good breeding. There was a strange smell in the room, partly perhaps of old wood, and partly of some chemical. May be Borgelt's own laboratory was somewhere quite close to this room. All the lights had been switched on, but that did little to dispel the gloom.

In a way, that was understandable, for there was nothing in the room whose colour might be described as pale. Every object was either a shade of brown or black. The atmosphere, on the whole, was both sombre and eerie.

Since I am a teetotaller, Borgelt offered me a glass of apple juice. The butler who brought the drinks on a tray, appeared to be about ninety years old. Perhaps because Borgelt caught me staring at him with surprise and wanted to satisfy my curiosity, he said, 'Rudi has been with our family for a long time—from even before I was born. His father and grandfather also served as butlers in this house.'

Borgelt's voice was not just deep, but had an unusual smooth texture, the like of which I had never heard before.

We raised our glasses and were drinking each other's health, when a telephone rang somewhere in the house. A little later, Rudi returned to say that it was a call for Paumer. Paumer got up and left the room.

Borgelt was also drinking apple juice. He twirled the glass in his hand and looked steadily at me. Then he said, 'Professor Shonku, I'm sure you are aware that scientists have been working for many years on the development of robots.'

'Yes, I am fully aware of that.'

'I too, have worked in this area.'

'Yes. I have read some of your articles.'

'The last article I wrote was ten years ago. My real research began *after* it was published. I haven't written a single word anywhere about my new research.'

I remained silent. Borgelt continued to stare at me through his sunken blue eyes. I could hear faint banging noises. They were coming from within the house, but were not very close. Why was Paumer taking so long? Who was he speaking to?

'Perhaps the call Paumer received was an urgent one,' said Borgelt. I gave a start. I had said nothing about Paumer. How had Borgelt guessed what I was thinking?

Before I could say anything however, Borgelt asked me a question that was completely unexpected.

'Will you sell your robot to me?'

Perfectly taken aback, I exclaimed, 'What! Why would you want to buy my robot?'

'Because I need it. There is only one reason for it. You see, the robot I built cannot handle mathematical problems. I need to rectify that. Urgently.'

'Is your robot here in this house?'

Borgelt nodded. The banging started again. That noise, coupled with the delay in Paumer's return, began to make me feel distinctly uneasy. However, at the same time, the thought that Borgelt's robot was in the same house, and that I might get to see it shortly, sent a shiver of excitement through my body.

Borgelt began speaking again. 'No one has been able to build a robot like mine. What I—Gottfried Borgelt—have created is totally unique. But my robot has one single drawback. It is not as quick as yours in doing calculations. If I could have your robot to work on, I could remove that one weakness from my own.'

This annoyed me no end. Would anyone part with an amazing creation just for money? It was the first robot I had built, with my own hands. Why should I sell it to a half-mad scientist in Heidelberg? It wasn't as if I was in dire need of money. Besides, it was my robot's mathematical prowess that made it so precious. That was my major achievement. It did not matter what claims Borgelt made about his own creation, I knew he could not have produced anything more astounding than mine.

'Forgive me, Borgelt,' I said, shaking my head, 'I cannot sell my robot. What I don't understand is why I should have to. If you are such a brilliant scientist, surely you can build an improved version like mine, if you try a little harder?'

'No,' Borgelt rose to his feet. 'We can't all do the same things, in the same way. That's the truth, that's the law of nature. Yes, if I tried hard enough, one day I could produce a flawless robot. I know that because there is nothing that I cannot do, if I put my mind to it. But I haven't got enough time. I have also lost virtually all my money. This house is mortgaged. I've spent all I had, in order to build that robot. Millions of Deutschmarks. Even so, it is not totally perfect. If I can correct that one fault, my own robot will help me earn those lost millions back. People will say—no, it is not humanly possible to do anything more than what Borgelt has done. I have some gold coins left in my safe. They are 400 years old. I will give you those. Sell me your robot.'

Borgelt had no idea that I had learnt a long time ago, to conquer temptation of any kind. But did he really think I would give up my precious creation for a few pieces of gold? When I spoke, my own voice sounded grave. 'I do not like your tone, Borgelt,' I said. 'I am *not* going to sell my robot, even if you offer me gold, or an entire diamond mine!'

'Then you leave me with no choice.'

So saying, Borgelt shut the door that led to a staircase and bolted it. Then he quickly walked over to the opposite end of the room and bolted the second door as well, which stood between the living and the dining room. The windows were already closed. The only door that now remained open, was the one that led to the library. That was where my Robu was standing. For the first time, the thought crossed my mind that perhaps I would never see him again. Soon, he might well be in the hands of a different master, and solve complex mathematical problems on his command. And Paumer? Now I was absolutely certain that Paumer and Borgelt were in this together. They had conspired to destroy me. . . .

Bang bang bang bang bang . . . I could hear that noise again. It seemed to be coming from the basement. Who was making it? Borgelt's robot?

There was no time to think. Borgelt was standing before me. His eyes held a vicious, cruel look—something I had never seen in the eyes of any other man.

When he spoke, I noticed that the smoothness had gone from his voice. It now sounded cold and hard as steel.

'Don't you know how much easier it is to destroy life than preserve it?' Borgelt's words echoed round the room. 'One electric shock is all that's needed. Do you know how many volts? Your Robu might know. And it's ever so easy to do it . . . !'

I was wearing a carbothene vest. It would protect

me from electric shocks, no matter how strong they were. I knew that. But how was I going to deal with the sheer physical strength of this German?

'Paumer! Paumer!' I shouted.

Borgelt was advancing towards me, his right arm outstretched, his fingers pointing at me. His eyes were shining with malicious glee. I tried to step back, but collided with a sofa. There was no space behind me.

Now Borgelt's fingers were only about six inches away from my forehead. Thoughts of Giridih began flashing through my mind . . .

Clang clang clang clang!

A sudden sound made me look right. Borgelt seemed to give a start, and turned his head. This was followed by an incredible, breathtaking event. Through the open door of the library emerged my own Robu. His eyes still had a squint; his lips still held a smile, exactly where I had put it.

He sped towards Borgelt like a hurricane, flashing steel everywhere, and flung his arms around him. What followed was as peculiar as it was horrible.

Robu appeared to be pressing Borgelt's head from both sides. Under such an impact, Borgelt's head twisted and turned, as if it had been screwed on. Then Robu pulled at it, until it came apart and fell on the floor with a clatter. Through the gap in his neck spilled out masses of electric wires.

I could no longer continue to stand. I fell on the sofa, almost unconscious. My vision blurred, my brain ceased to think.

Hovering on the brink of unconsciousness, I could hear someone banging on the door that faced the staircase. 'Shonku! Open the door. Come on, open the door!'

It was Paumer's voice. All at once, life returned to my limbs, my vision cleared. I ran to the door and opened it. On the other side stood three men: Paumer, Rudi and—yes, now there could be no mistake—the real Gottfried Borgelt, the scientist.

*

There is nothing much left to tell. The questions that rose in my mind were answered by Paumer before I could ask any.

'On your first night, it was I who went into the laboratory and fitted some extra gadgets into your robot's head,' explained Paumer. 'Those gadgets were my own inventions. As a result, a telepathic link was made between your mind and his. That's what alerted him when you were in danger. That is why he could no longer remain silent and passive.'

Borgelt said, 'A robot ought to remain a robot. I mean, it should simply be a machine, no more. When I built my own robot, I made it so much like myself, and gave it so many human qualities, that it began to resent its own creator. It simply didn't want another being to be present who was exactly like him. I had wanted it to carry on with my work when I died. But the human brain is such a complex affair—no man can re-create it, or predict how it's going to behave. The minute I completed the finishing touches and released my look-alike, he immediately captured me! But he didn't kill me because he knew that, if anything went wrong, no one but I could save him.'

'Rudi,' Paumer put in, 'knew everything. But he was too scared to do anything by himself. So he pretended that the telephone call was for me. He thought that if he could get me to come outside, he and I could go down to the basement together and rescue Borgelt. We didn't realize that your own life would be threatened before we returned!'

Suddenly, a new thought dawned upon me; and it filled me with joy. 'Now do you see why my Robu didn't tell us Borgelt's name in Paumer's house?' I asked. 'How could he, when the person asking him wasn't the real Borgelt? Neither Paumer nor I realized that we were speaking to a mechanized look-alike. But Robu knew. Perhaps it takes one machine to know another!'

Translated by Gopa Majumdar

Professor Shonku and the Egyptian Terror

7 September

I am writing my diary in room number 5 of the Hotel Imperial in Port Said. It is now 11.30 p.m. Perhaps people here are used to late nights, for through an open window, I can hear the hum of traffic and other noises from the city. Until about ten o'clock, it had felt quite sultry. But now, there is a light, cool breeze that seems to be coming from the Suez Canal.

I have no idea if my visit to Egypt is going to be successful, but today's events have been quite encouraging. I had wanted to visit Egypt for a long time. As a matter of fact, I think every scientist should come to Egypt. The scientific knowledge and skill that Egyptians showed as many as five thousand years ago is truly astounding. Be it in chemistry, mathematics or medicine—the ancient Egyptians had reached extraordinary levels of sophistication all those years ago.

What I find most amazing are Egyptian mummies. Egyptians used to chemically treat the dead bodies of important people, and wrap them up in bandages in such a way that, even five thousand years later, when those bandages were taken off, the corpse appeared perfectly preserved without any sign of decay. No modern scientist has yet been able to unravel the mystery behind this technique of preservation of mummies.

I had heard before I left Giridih that a British archaeologist, Dr James Summerton, was excavating in the Bubastis region in Egypt. Having read all of Summerton's books on Egypt, I wanted to meet that archaeological team, right from the start. It was Summerton who had carried out excavations in the Sahara for three years, and discovered that amazing chamber belonging to Kheratape, a king from the fourth dynasty.

Who knew that I would get to meet Summerton, so unexpectedly, within a few hours of my arrival here?

In the morning, as soon as I had checked into the hotel, I had gone to see the manager to make enquiries about Summerton. When I found him, he was reading a newspaper. My question made him raise his eyes from his paper. 'Why, are you after the same thing?' he asked.

I did not like his tone. 'What do you mean?' I countered.

'Well, if you've come here with the same intention, I consider it my duty to warn you. Or else you might meet with the same fate as Summerton.'

'Why, what's happened to him?'

'Punishment. Just desserts, that's what's happened to him. He had the gall to dig into the earth and then enter an ancient tomb. He had no right to do that! And now he's paying for it, but perhaps he won't have to suffer for long. Very few people survive if they're bitten by a scarab beetle.'

I had read about scarab beetles. In ancient Egypt, it was worshipped as a manifestation of a god.

Further questions elicited some more information: yesterday, in Bubastis, while the excavation was in progress, Summerton is said to have screamed suddenly and fallen to the ground. His companions rushed to him and found him clutching his right calf, his face twisted in pain. 'That beetle! That beetle!' he was heard muttering.

No one could find the insect.

Summerton was rushed to the hospital in Port Said. His condition was believed to be serious.

When I heard that, I decided not to waste another minute. I left for the hospital at once, taking with me the medicine I have invented, called Miracurol. Back in India, the same medicine has helped innumerable people bitten by kraits, cobras and scorpions. Just one dose usually has a miraculous effect.

When I finally saw Summerton in the hospital, he was truly in bad shape. But obviously, he had enormous will power. In spite of all the discomfort, he was lying quietly in his bed. His face was twisting from time to time—the only indication of the intense pain he must have been suffering.

I introduced myself and told him that I had come to see him briefly, simply as a devoted reader of his works. To my surprise, he seemed to recognize my name. In fact, he told me—speaking in a faint voice—that he too, had read many of my books and one in particular, was his favourite. It was a book on all the original studies I had made of spirits and spectres.

Perhaps because of this, he seemed prepared to trust me and took a dose of Miracurol without the slightest objection.

When I got back to my hotel, it was half past eleven. Around 3 p.m., I received a message from the hospital to say that Summerton was feeling a lot better. He had no fever, his colour had returned to normal, and the pain was considerably reduced. I have no doubt that by tomorrow, he will be completely recovered. I must see him then, and ask him if he will let me join him just for a few days.

8 September, midnight

I went to the hospital quite early this morning. As I had expected, Summerton was fully restored to health. The bite mark left by the beetle had disappeared miraculously, as had the last traces of pain. I myself was surprised by the effects of my medicine. It was made of some really weird ingredients! I did not tell Summerton anything about those. If he heard the details, especially about the whiskers taken from lobsters, he would certainly have taken me to be completely crazy. As things stand, he is extremely grateful to me. I did not have to raise the subject of joining his team. Summerton himself invited me. Naturally, I accepted immediately.

It turned out that Summerton is also most intrigued by Egyptian mummies. But he does believe that if he, or someone from his team, enters an ancient tomb and disturbs its contents, then they may incur the wrath of some Egyptian god or other, and become the victim of a curse. The beetle that bit him, Summerton is convinced, was a scarab. He is currently working on a site where they have found a temple. Apparently, the figure of a scarab beetle is carved on one of its walls. I knew that thousands of years ago, Egyptians used to worship various animals, fish and birds as incarnations of gods and goddesses. I said to Summerton, 'I believe a tomb was found somewhere which contained the mummy of a cat?'

'Yes, it was found in Bubastis, the same place where I am working. But it is not a recent discovery, and it isn't just one cat. About a hundred cats were mummified and put in coffins; then they were all placed in that tomb. A cat was supposed to be an incarnation of the goddess Nephdet.'

I decided to visit this strange tomb, if I could find the time and opportunity. I love cats. I had to leave my own Newton at home. I feel homesick whenever I think of him.

*

By the time I returned to the hotel after my meeting with Summerton, the sun had risen quite high and it felt warm. As I got closer to the entrance to my hotel, a local man stepped forward and approached me. He was very tall—certainly over six feet. His skin was a shade of burnt copper, his curly hair was cut very short, and his eyes were sunken. The look in them was sharp and ruthless.

He placed a rough hand on my shoulder most rudely. Then he stared at me for a few seconds, before saying, 'You appear to be an Indian. So why are you getting mixed up with these white brutes? Why are you so concerned about the ancient and holy objects of our past?'

I made no attempt to hide my annoyance. 'What if I am?' I said, just as roughly, 'What's wrong with showing an interest? Does it automatically mean that I am being disrespectful? Do you have any idea how much respect I have for ancient Egyptian civilization?'

The man's eyes seemed to light up. His hand was still on my shoulder. He pressed my shoulder with it. 'Interest is one thing,' he said, 'but digging the earth, then stepping into the sacred resting place of a departed soul and disturbing its peace, is quite another. Do you know where Mr Summerton is working?'

'Yes. In a tomb dating back to the time of a king who belonged to the fourth dynasty of rulers in Bubastis.'

'And are you aware that that is where my own ancestors are buried?'

I burst out laughing. 'Really? So you know about ancestors who lived several hundred generations ago?'

This seemed to infuriate the man even further. He shook me this time. 'You will find out how much I know, if you visit that excavation site and go into that temple!'

With these words, he suddenly released me and strode back to the main road. Soon, he was lost in the crowd. I heaved a sigh of relief and returned to my room.

Summerton will restart work tomorrow, and I will go with him. So I had better pack my things, I thought. I couldn't help feeling excited, just as I had when I'd gone to the Nilgiris to look for the bones of a prehistoric animal.

A tomb dedicated to cats! The very thought made me smile.

Tomorrow, I must tell Summerton about my encounter with that tall, impertinent, half-mad character. The truth of the matter, I think, is quite simple. When an ancient temple is excavated, very often archaeologists find valuable jewellery studded with precious stones. Many local people are aware of this. Some might think that an archaeologist can be threatened or frightened into parting with some of his findings. If that man causes any more trouble, I have decided to use my Snuff-gun on him. Luckily, I have brought it with me. If I aim it at his nose and pull the trigger, he will sneeze non-stop for two days. After that, it will be interesting to see if he comes back to annoy me again.

10 September

We reached Bubastis yesterday morning. In the afternoon, I went down with Summerton to see the recently dug burial chamber that was said to be 4000 years old. It evoked a feeling that is very hard to describe. I had to climb down a narrow flight of stairs and pass through a narrower passage in order to enter the chamber. According to Summerton, it was the burial chamber of some important nobleman. In the centre of a large hall, stood an ornately carved wooden sarcophagus. Around the main chamber were smaller chambers, each containing a sarcophagus of its own. The bodies those held were probably those of officials or followers close to the nobleman. The Egyptians used to believe that the soul of a dead person lingered around the body, and still required the same objects that the person was wont to use when he—or she—was alive. Food had been laid out on plates and kept near the sarcophagus; wine was stored in barrels; and there were clothes, toiletries, even ancient sports equipment.

Summerton lifted the lid of a sarcophagus and offered me a glimpse of the mummy in it. Its arms were folded and the hands placed across the chest. From head to toe, it was wrapped in bandage. A pungent smell greeted me as soon as the lid was lifted. I stared at the mummy in speechless wonder. I had read so much about mummies. Who knew that, one day, I would be looking down at one?

On the mummy's chest was a piece of paper with something written in hieroglyphics. It was no ordinary paper. The writing was on a sheet of four-thousand year-old papyrus. Summerton could read the language—though, of course, it was not something one could read quickly and easily like a modern language. 'That papyrus explains who the dead man was,' Summerton told me, 'It doesn't just give his name. It also tells you when and how he died.'

We spent the whole day inspecting the chambers. When finally we began our journey back to our camp in the evening, Summerton suddenly asked me, 'You believe that ghosts and spirits and all things supernatural have a scientific basis, don't you? At least, that's the impression I got from your books.'

'Yes,' I replied, 'that's true. But I also believe that there are still certain issues which science cannot explain. Dreams, for instance. No scientist has been able to explain fully why we dream. Maybe in another twenty, fifty, or hundred years, this situation will change. Every mystery in the world will have been solved by science. That is what I believe, anyway.'

Summerton grew thoughtful. After a pause, he said, 'People here seem to think that the soul of every corpse in those chambers is displeased because we have disturbed its peace. All those dead people are cursing us. Maybe one day we will have to face the consequences.'

These words made me smile, for they reminded me of that lunatic. When I told Summerton about him, he too, began laughing. 'That man,' he said, 'has been badgering me from the start. He threatened me as well. I'm sure he'd leave us alone if we paid him some money.'

'Then why don't you? At least you could then work in peace.'

Summerton shook his head. 'No, I have no wish to waste any money on a petty criminal. If I give in, I know he'll become more greedy. We must think of other archaeologists who might work here in the future, mustn't we? If we ignore the man completely, he'll soon realize there's nothing doing, and he'll make himself scarce.'

On our return to the camp, I had a glass of cold sherbet, which was most refreshing. Then I found a canvas chair and sat outside my tent. To the west stood the pyramid of Giza, looking dark and grey against the setting sun. Here was another mystery. No one knew how it had been possible to build this pyramid in those ancient times.

To the north was a row of date palms. On one of those, perched very still, were three vultures. There was a time when even vultures were worshipped in Egypt as incarnations of a god. The Egyptians were really a most intriguing race.

12 September

Today, Summerton made me an offer that was profoundly startling. It told me how grateful he was to me, for having saved his life.

We were on our way back to the camp after a whole day spent in the tomb devoted to cats. 'Shonku,' said Summerton, blowing smoke out of his pipe, 'You know, I was puzzling over what I could do in return for what you did for me. Today, I have had an idea, but I need to know how you feel about it.'

Summerton paused for breath. It was clear that he was still quite weak after his encounter with the scarab beetle. We walked on in silence. After a few minutes, he spoke again, 'You want to do research on mummies, don't you? Suppose I gave you one of the mummies I've found here. Would you like that, or not?'

I was so completely taken aback by this offer that, for a few seconds, I could not speak at all. Return home with a mummy of my own for my experiments? It was something I hadn't even dreamt of. I swallowed hard and forced myself to speak. 'If I could take a mummy back with me, I would consider my visit to Egypt entirely successful, and of course I would remain eternally grateful to you.'

Summerton smiled. 'What would you like—a cat or a man?'

To be honest, purely from a scientific point of view, it did not matter which mummy I got to work on. But when I thought of my sweet, harmless Newton, I did not feel like choosing the mummy of a cat. Newton often wanders around my laboratory. Heaven knows how he'll react if he finds a four-thousand-year-old feline body in there. So I said, 'I'd prefer a man.'

Summerton said, 'Very well. But if you must take a human mummy, take something interesting. I have discovered a new burial chamber, not far from the one that has all those cats. This one has got about thirty bodies. We don't yet know who those men were. I have a feeling there is some mystery attached to their deaths. The hieroglyphics explaining the cause of death are of a special kind; I have not yet been able to fully grasp their meaning. Tell you what, I'll give you one of those mummies, but I will keep the papyrus. When I get back home, I am going to read the whole thing carefully, and then I'll let you know what I find. In the meantime, you can carry on with your research, and keep me informed. If you can unearth the mystery behind the chemicals used on mummies, you may even get the Nobel Prize, who knows?'

I do not need to stay in Egypt any longer. If I can get that mummy—so kindly donated by Summerton—and have it packed and placed on a homebound ship, my heart's desire will be fulfilled. Then I will have all the time in the world to do my research. I have to admit Summerton is really most generous. Perhaps it is not unusual for one scientist to feel a bond with another, although they may be from different countries. I have known Summerton for only three days, but feel as if we've been friends for years.

15 September

I returned to Port Said today, and had to deal with a most awkward situation as soon as I reached my hotel. Close to it was a large shop, from which I had just bought a leather briefcase and stepped out, when I came face to face with that same tall madman. He grabbed me by my collar at once. I was too taken aback to say or do anything. So much had happened since my conversation with Summerton that I had totally forgotten about the man. Since I was not expecting to be attacked, I was not carrying any of my weapons, either.

The man bent over my face. His eyes were bloodshot. 'I warned you, didn't I?' he hissed, 'But you didn't listen to me. You are going to take the body of one of my ancestors to your country. You cannot imagine the retribution that will fall upon you. I will settle scores with you myself. Yes, your punishment will come from these hands!'

He tightened his grip on my neck and would probably have tried to choke me, but at that moment a policeman in the street saw what he was doing and rushed forward to stop him. A few passers-by had also stopped to come to my aid. The lunatic was restrained by the policeman. 'He's completely crazy,' explained a passer-by, looking at me sympathetically, 'He's been arrested many times, but he comes back here every time he is released and starts making trouble again.'

The policeman assured me that the man would trouble me no more. The police would make sure of that.

To be honest, I was not really worried. I already had a reservation on a ship going to India in just two days. With me, would go the four-thousand-year-old mummy that Summerton had given me. When I got home, my first priority would be to unwrap its bandage and start my research. I must solve the chemical mystery behind Egyptian mummies.

17 September

I am once again in a ship sailing down the Red Sea. The sea is rough, but I do not mind. My only problem is that I cannot hold the pen straight, and so writing is difficult. The sarcophagus, suitably packed, is lying in the cargo section of the ship. I can't stop thinking about it.

Summerton came to the port to say goodbye. I reminded him to let me know as soon as he finished reading the words on the papyrus. I also invited him to visit Giridih if he could find the time, and stay with me as my guest.

Just as the ship started pulling out, my eyes fell on a face in the crowd waiting on land. The man was taller than any other. I peered through my binoculars for a better look. Yes, it was the same man, staring straight at me. His lips were spread in a thin, cruel smile. His eyes held the same cold, harsh look. Perhaps the police had failed to keep him inside a prison.

The Red Sea is getting increasingly restless. I must stop writing.

27 September

I reached Giridih this morning. It was Prahlad's startled glance that suddenly made me aware that I had come back considerably darker and sunburnt. Later, the mirror in my room simply confirmed this.

Newton greeted me warmly, by rubbing his head on my trousers and purring gently. Thank goodness I did not bring a feline mummy. Newton would never have accepted it.

The sarcophagus has taken up a lot of space in my laboratory. I was getting so impatient that I had it taken out of the packing case.

As a matter of fact, I looked at the sarcophagus properly only when it was unpacked. Its lid was beautifully carved. One look at it told me of the expertise of Egyptian craftsmen.

I lifted the lid. Inside was another box shaped like a human figure. What it meant was that this box was a simple replica of its occupant. A face—complete with eyes, nose and a mouth—was painted on it. The rest of the box was covered with colourful designs, created with a paint brush.

I removed the lid of the second box and was immediately greeted by that same familiar smell. Then I looked at the body inside. Like all other mummies, this one was buried under layers of bandage, and its hands were placed on its chest. I could not see its face; but it was easy enough to see that the man had been very

HCl
H2SO4

tall, perhaps more than six feet.

From tomorrow, I will start removing the bandage. Today I am feeling very tired. Besides, I must clean all my research equipment. In my absence, they have gathered considerable dust and sand, blown from the river.

Also, tomorrow I am going to get Avinash Babu to take a look at that sarcophagus and its contents. Maybe he will stop making snide remarks about my scientific work, at least for a few days. Only a little while ago, I heard a noise that sounded as if someone was banging on the front door. I thought it was Avinash Babu, and sent Prahlad to open the door. But Prahlad returned and told me that there was no one there. Perhaps it was simply the wind. It has been wet and windy over the last few days, I hear.

29 September

I was in no state to write my diary after what happened yesterday. So I am now trying to record—as coherently as I can—everything that happened.

I had ended my last entry with mention of the wind making a funny noise at my front door. We had a storm that evening, but it stopped at around 11 p.m. I fell asleep soon after that. Later in the night, however, I was woken by the same sound of someone banging on the front door.

Prahlad sleeps in the corridor outside my room. Whatever his virtues, Prahlad has one major fault. Once he is asleep, he is dead to the world. That banging noise, I saw, had done nothing to wake him. So I picked up a torch myself, and went down to see who had arrived at my door so late at night.

I opened the front door, but could find no one. I shone my torch outside. There was no one to be seen. Suddenly, my hand moved accidentally and the light fell on the steps that lead to the front verandah. On them were damp footprints. The size of those made me feel faintly uneasy. Who in Giridih could have such huge feet?

But there was no point in worrying about it. Whoever it was, had vanished. I could only hope that having beaten his retreat, the fellow would not reappear again in the dead of night.

I locked the front door and returned to my bedroom. But some odd instinct made me leave it again and go to my laboratory. To my relief, I found that everything was in place. I could spot nothing suspicious or out of the ordinary. The sarcophagus was where it had been placed, and its lid was firmly shut.

When I came out of the lab, I found Newton cowering in one corner of the passage outside. All his hair was standing on end, and he appeared really tense. Obviously, like me, he wasn't used to being woken in the middle of the night by strange noises. It had clearly disturbed him.

I picked him up in my arms and went back to my bedroom. Then I shut the door, put Newton down on the carpet beside my bed, and went back to sleep.

In the morning—yesterday, that is—I rose early, had a cup of coffee and went straight to the laboratory. It took me two hours to clean all the glass apparatus. Test-tubes, jars, bottles and flasks—all were coated with dust.

Then I told Prahlad not to let anyone come into the house until I re-emerged from the lab; nor was he to enter the room himself without prior warning.

Having thus instructed Prahlad, I set to work. All my equipment was laid out on a table next to the sarcophagus. I dragged a chair, sat down and turned my attention to the mummy. Among the chemicals used by Egyptians to prevent a corpse from decaying, there were such things as sodium hydroxide, bitumen, balsam and honey. But, in addition to those, they used various other substances which have not yet been successfully analysed and identified by any scientist. It was those mysterious constituents that I had to uncover.

I looked closely at the mummy. The body itself was probably still intact, but in the last four thousand years, the bandages had not escaped undamaged. I would have to use tongs and tweezers and lift them very carefully.

I donned a pair of gloves and a mask, and began my work, starting from the top of the body.

What was exposed first of all was the forehead, followed by the remaining face. The forehead was not very wide. The eyes were deep-set. The nose was long and sharp. But what was that on the right cheek? There were three long, vertical scars. As if some sharp object had torn the flesh open. Could it be a battle wound, caused by a sword? But if that was the case, why should there be three scars, and why should they run parallel to one another?

As I got closer to revealing the mouth, suddenly the face began to appear familiar. Those jaws, those eyes, and that nose . . . where had I seen them before?

Yes. The face of the mummy bore a startling resemblance to that of the lunatic in Port Said.

But that was not really so amazing, was it? Bengalis might be a most diverse race—two unrelated men rarely look similar. But the Egyptians are different. One Egyptian frequently looks like another. In fact, the features one may find on statues of ancient men and women, can be spotted on modern Egyptians roaming the streets of Port Said. There was nothing startling about it. That crazy man obviously had features that were typical of his race.

What had he said to me? 'You are carrying the body of one of my own ancestors!' I had probably paid those words more attention than they deserved. That was the only reason why this face here—now fully exposed—was causing me vague unease.

I forced myself to stop thinking about the man in Port Said and concentrate on my work. As I began working on the neck, it became clear that the bandage had rotted away. The slightest pull made it disintegrate into pieces. But I knew that it would not do to lose my patience and pull faster. So I continued to work slowly and steadily.

So absorbed was I in my work that I totally lost track of time. It was only when it began to get dark that I realized I would have to stop, if only to switch the light on. So I put my tools down and was about to rise from my chair when, suddenly, my eyes fell on the window. What I saw sent a cold shiver down my spine.

Staring through the glass pane, his face pressed against it, was that madman from Port Said. The look in his eyes was now a hundred times more vicious than before. He was looking alternately at me and the box that held the mummy.

Perhaps if I switched the light on, I would feel less confused, I thought. So I raised a hand to press the switch. In the same instant, the man pushed so hard against the window that the bolt on it broke, and he burst into the room. Then he began advancing towards me, his arms outstretched, his eyes gleaming with devilish glee. Not once did he remove his gaze from my face.

I cannot describe, in any detail, what followed. It happened in a flash, before I could grasp anything. Just as the man was close enough to lunge forward and attack me, Newton turned up from nowhere. With a furious hiss, he sprang up in the air and landed directly on the man's face.

This unexpected attack made the man reel backward and fall to the floor. Within seconds, streams of blood were flowing down his cheek. I could scarcely believe my eyes. Newton had never displayed such aggression.

The odd thing was that once he'd fallen, the man could not rise to his feet again. Newton had killed him. Perhaps the shock of that attack was so great that it had caused heart failure. I could think of no other reason for his sudden death.

As soon as the man breathed his last, Newton calmed down and left the laboratory like a good boy. And, immediately, a most unpleasant smell made me glance quickly at the mummy. Signs of decay were now evident. The ancient Egyptian magic had come to an end, just as life had been snuffed out of the man from Port Said.

I moved swiftly. Without wasting another moment, I shut the lid of the smaller box and then that of the sarcophagus. Then I sprayed the room with the freshener I had made myself. It contained the fragrance of thirty-six different flowers.

The mystery behind the preservation of mummies, I guess, will now remain unsolved. In this matter, some unknown ancient Egyptian scientist will always remain one-up on even the most talented scientist in modern India.

The local police arrived as soon as I sent for them. Inspector Jatin Samaddar is well known to me. He surveyed the scene with open amazement. 'Well,' he said finally, 'no one can hold you responsible for that body in the wooden box. But . . . that fellow lying on the floor may well cause you some trouble. I mean, you will have to help us with our investigation, sir, and answer a lot of questions.'

'Very well. I will help you in any way I can. For the moment, please do me a favour and have these bodies removed. I mean the ancient one as well as the modern!'

7 October

I heard from Summerton today. In his letter, he said:

> Dear Professor Shonku,
>
> I hope you have made some progress towards getting that Nobel Prize. I have at last been able to read what was written on the papyrus that we found with your mummy. It describes who the dead man was, and then it says, 'He was given a death sentence because

he insulted Nephdet, the goddess with the face of a cat. However, before the order could be carried out, a cat scratched his face and he lost his life most mysteriously.' It means that the goddess herself punished him by appearing in the form of a cat. Isn't that strange? Could it have a scientific explanation? Think about it.

Let me know how you are getting on. I have been telling everyone in Britain about my encounter with that beetle, and how you saved my life.

Yours truly,
James Summerton

I finished reading the letter, folded it and was in the process of putting back in the envelope, when I felt Newton rubbing his face on my trouser leg. I picked him up, placed him on my lap and asked affectionately, 'Tell me, my dear cat, are *you* an incarnation of an Egyptian goddess?'

'Meaow,' said Newton.

Translated by Gopa Majumdar

Professor Shonku and the Curious Statuettes

12 May

Today is a memorable day in my life. The Swedish Academy of Science conferred a doctorate on me, thereby making all my hard work over the last five years truly worthwhile. My research was to do with crossbreeding one kind of fruit with another. In the end, the fruit I produced was more attractive, sweet-smelling and tasty than any other ever seen or tasted before.

Last year, the Swedish scientist, Svendsen, came to my laboratory in Giridih. He was quite speechless after he'd eaten one of my creations. Upon his return to Sweden, he wrote widely about my work. As a result, the matter received a lot of publicity abroad. In fact, Svendsen is responsible, to a large extent, for the honour that I received today. My heart fills with gratitude towards him as I write my diary.

This is my first visit to Sweden. It is a beautiful, neat and tidy country. Since it is the month of May, there is daylight round the clock. But the sun looks dull and isn't very warm. It seems as if it's about to set, no matter what time of day it is. I wonder how people cope when, in the winter, the night becomes never-ending. I have heard that some people here are so moved by the first sight of the sun that, overpowered by their emotions, they go and kill themselves! Those of us who live closer to the equator are probably better off. There is no reason to envy people who live in the north, in cold countries.

I have been thinking of going to Norway from here. There is a particular reason for it. Four years ago when I visited England, I came to know, quite closely, the famous zoologist, Professor Archibald Ackroyd. I spent a weekend in his cottage in Sussex. At the time, Ackroyd was on the point of going to Norway to study a certain species of rodent called 'lemmings'. From what I have heard, these are extraordinary creatures. At a particular time every year, thousands of lemmings come out of forests and travel towards the sea. On their way, they are attacked by jackals, wolves and eagles. But that does nothing to stop them. When finally, they reach the sea, they simply jump into the water, knowing that they would be drowned.

Ackroyd's study probably remained incomplete. I read in the papers after my return to Giridih that Ackroyd died while he was in Norway. Could I possibly find what Ackroyd had set out to seek? It is this thought that makes me want to travel to Norway.

A few minutes after I returned to my hotel room, having had dinner, someone knocked on my door. I was still thinking of lemmings. I opened the door to find a tall, middle-aged man. His hair was blond, his glasses were set in a golden frame and, behind the thick lenses, were a pair of sharp blue eyes. When he parted his lips in a smile and introduced himself, I saw that he had one gold tooth. His name was Gregor Lindquist, he said. He lived in Sulitjelma in Norway, and was an artist. He made statuettes of famous people. The skin colour, hair, nails and clothes on each figure were always exactly like the real person's—but the statuette was never more than six inches tall.

He told me all this and exchanged pleasantries for a few minutes, then came to the point, somewhat hesitantly. 'If you could visit me in Norway for a few days and stay with me as my guest, I'd be delighted,' he said. 'That would give me the chance to create a statuette to look like you. There is no famous Indian in my collection, you see. If you agree, I should consider it a special privilege.'

We continued to chat. After a while, I couldn't help telling him of my interest in lemmings. At this, Lindquist offered to get hold of a lemming and show it to me in his house, before I decided to go off into the forests to look for them. After this, there was really nothing left to be said.

I have agreed to go to Norway with Mr Lindquist. We leave next Thursday.

17 May

I arrived in Sulitjelma two days ago. This very pleasant city is in the Kjolen valley, in northern Norway. There are copper mines here, and to the west, stand the Sulitjelma mountains, rising to more than 6000 feet. Compared to our Himalayan peaks, they are little more than hillocks. But, in Norway, they contain the country's second highest peak.

Lindquist is looking after me extremely well. His house is in an isolated spot, there are no other houses nearby. As it is, Norway is a thinly populated country. Even in such a place, Lindquist seems to have found a particularly remote area to live in. I have no problem with that. When I built my own house in Giridih, I also chose a quiet locality.

I haven't yet seen a lemming. Lindquist asked me to give him a couple of days to find one. I have no problem with that either, for I am in no pressing hurry to return home. What I need right now is rest and relaxation. Here, I am getting to eat plenty of fresh trout and excellent cheese. On the whole, I am enjoying myself a great deal.

There is just one thing about Lindquist that occasionally makes me feel uncomfortable. He keeps staring at me. If someone looks at me while we are talking, that is perfectly natural. But even when we are both silent, Lindquist gazes at me steadily, without blinking. This morning, I couldn't take it any more and asked him why he was doing that. Lindquist answered my question without the slightest trace of embarrassment. 'If I can study my subject thoroughly before I start to make a statuette, my job becomes a lot easier. Then I do not require the subject to stand or sit still for me for hours on end.'

I couldn't help asking another question. 'When will you show me your statuettes? I am most curious.'

'They have gathered dust. Tomorrow, my servant Hans will clean them. I should be able to show them to you in the evening.'

'And the lemming?'

'First, the statuettes. Then the lemming. All right?'

I had to agree.

18 May, midnight

I have been back in my room for two hours, but am still feeling so excited that I find it difficult to write—with any measure of coherence—all that happened today.

This evening, at around 7 p.m. (I am calling it 'evening' because that is the time my watch showed. Here it is impossible to distinguish between morning and evening), Lindquist opened a secret door in his living room and took me down a spiral staircase. In his basement was his collection of statuettes. I had never seen anything like them.

The tiny figures that I saw, placed under glass lids, were so lifelike that I hesitate to refer to them as statuettes. The only difference between each figure and a real person was that the figure was inanimate, and no more than six inches in height. That meant that each was about one-tenth of the size of a normal human being.

There were six figures in all. Each was based on someone famous, although until now, I had no idea how some of them looked. Among those that I recognized, were the French traveller, Henri Clemeau, and the black champion boxer, Bob Sleeman.

The statuette in the last glass 'cage', wearing dark glasses and standing with his right hand stuffed into his pocket, was my friend, the late Archibald Ackroyd—the zoologist who died two years ago here in Norway, while looking for lemmings.

One look at Ackroyd's statuette told me how perfectly made it was. Not only were its features identical to those of the real man, but it was made with a substance that made its hair, skin and eyes look perfectly natural.

It nearly took my breath away. Lindquist saw me standing still before Ackroyd's figure and asked, 'What's the matter? Did you know him?'

'Yes. I knew him very well. I met him in England. It was he who told me about lemmings. Then I heard that he died in Norway.'

'Yes, he did. I have to say I was extremely lucky because only a few days before his death, he visited me and I was able to create that statuette. Each one of these men whose figures you see here visited me in my house and sat for me.'

We went back up the same staircase and returned to the living room. 'From the day after tomorrow,' Lindquist told me, 'I will start on your statuette.'

Even as I am writing this down, Ackroyd's smiling face is coming back to me every now and then. I could not have imagined that anyone could produce such a completely lifelike figure. Was Lindquist only an artist? Or was he perhaps also a scientist? What material did he use to make those figures? I hope when he builds mine, he will do so in my presence, so that I get the chance to see the material myself.

Tomorrow morning, I will try asking him a few questions. Let's see what he says. I think I will stop worrying about lemmings for the moment, and concentrate on Lindquist's statuettes.

19 May

Last night, my sleep was disturbed by a sudden gust of wind that brought with it a sharp, pungent smell. It hung in the air for a long time. Something familiar was mixed with the scent of some unknown object. What I could recognize were copper sulphate and ferrous oxide. The overall smell was a bit sweet and cloying. It could have been a chemical, or something quite different. What I am sure of, is that somebody is working either in this house, or very close to it, using a number of chemicals. Lindquist must be a scientist.

In the morning, Lindquist's old servant, Hans, came and told me, 'My master has gone out. He would like you to have your breakfast, he said. There is no need to wait for him.'

After breakfast, I had a stroll in the compound and around the house. I saw pieces of scientific apparatus strewn carelessly behind bushes. There were pieces of broken test-tubes, flasks and an old Bunsen burner. Now there was no doubt in my mind that science had played a role in creating those statuettes. My eyes could not be so easily deceived.

There is only one thought that keeps bothering me. If Lindquist is a scientist, why should he not admit that to a fellow scientist? Why should he want to be known purely as an artist?

I went back inside at around half past nine. There was still no sign of Lindquist. Hans had no idea when he might be back. I sat alone in my room for a while; then a cunning idea occurred to me. What if I went and had another look at those statuettes, this time just by myself?

The secret door in the living room had to be opened in a special way. I had seen Lindquist twist its handle a few times to the right, then to the left, and give one final pull before it swung open. I had memorised the technique. I don't think an ordinary person could have done it.

I called Hans. 'Look,' I said, 'I need to send an urgent telegram. Could you please send it for me? You see, I am feeling a little breathless, it must be your cold climate. Now I'm afraid to walk all the way to the post office.'

Hans agreed to go at once, and I wrote a totally unnecessary telegram, addressing it to Prahlad in Giridih. Then I gave Hans some money, and he left.

I waited another five minutes before going out and standing at the front gate. If I looked in either direction, I could see quite a long distance. Lindquist was nowhere to be seen. Even if he was on his way home, he was not going to be back for another fifteen minutes.

I went back inside and found the right door in the living room. Then I twisted its handle the same way as Lindquist, and a few seconds later, it opened with a click. I had a torch in my pocket. I switched it on, climbed down to the basement and entered the room where all the statuettes were displayed.

When I shone the torch on every glass cage, I could spot no difference. In the first cage was the Italian singer. I think his name was Mario Batista. In the second was the boxer, Bob Sleeman. Other cages contained the French traveller, Henri Clemeau; the Japanese swimmer, Hakimoto; the German poet whose name I could not remember; and, in the sixth and final cage, was my friend, Ackroyd.

I grasped the torch firmly and went closer to Ackroyd's cage. The glass cages were specially designed. At one glance, they appeared no different from the lids that are sometimes placed over expensive clocks and statues. But these had little doors that could be locked and unlocked. However, it was possible to lift the whole lid, if one so wished, in which case it did not matter if the door remained locked.

I pressed my face against the glass to get a closer look at Ackroyd's figure. In a few moments, it began to appear as if the way he was standing was slightly different from the way I had seen him stand yesterday. His right hand was thrust more deeply into his pocket. But could it be just my imagination? Maybe the limbs of those figures were flexible and could be moved? Maybe Lindquist opened the door of each cage at times and changed the position of the figures. Or perhaps arms and legs were re-positioned accidentally when the figures were dusted and cleaned. Why didn't I see for myself?

I could have picked up Ackroyd, but felt awkward at the thought. So I removed the lid that covered the Japanese swimmer, and picked him up gingerly. It became obvious at once that Lindquist had left no flexibility in his limbs. His whole body was stiff and lifeless.

I replaced the lid, and returned to the living room via the spiral staircase and the secret door. Then I simply went to my own room and waited there.

Lindquist came back at half past twelve. Over lunch, I said to him, 'I'd like to do a bit of reading today. I believe you have a good public library here. Could I go there?'

'Easily. I'll tell you how to get there. I suggest you go today, because from tomorrow, you are going to be busy sitting for me.'

I went to the library straight after lunch, without bothering to have a rest. A vague suspicion had raised its head in my mind. I had to look at old press reports to see if that suspicion was justified.

I spent three and a half hours in the library, looking at old copies of the *London Times*. Then I returned home, my mind filled with grave disquiet, agitation and anxiety. The first thing I looked at, was a report on Ackroyd's death. Two years ago, on 11 September, the *London Times* reported that no one knew exactly how Ackroyd had died. All that was known was that he went missing in Norway. He was last seen getting into a boat to go across the fjord. That boat was never seen again, so everyone assumed that it had capsized and Ackroyd had been killed.

Then I read about the deaths of Bob Sleeman, Henri Clemeau and Hakimoto. Each went missing in Europe. Several attempts were made in each case to find the man, to no avail. In the end, they were all presumed dead.

Upon my return, I said nothing to Lindquist and tried to behave normally. I had almost stopped thinking about lemmings.

When we sat down to have dinner, Lindquist said, 'Don't you ever drink, Shonku? I have some really good Norwegian wine. I don't like it myself, but other people seem to love it. Have a taste.'

I did not want Lindquist to get even remotely suspicious about what was on my mind, so I raised no objection.

Lindquist poured some wine into a glass. As I raised it to my lips, I could smell something distinctly odd. Even so, I took a small sip and quickly spat it out on my napkin. 'Sorry,' I said, 'I'm afraid I don't like it at all. In this matter, our taste seems to be the same. Why don't you give me some of that stuff you are drinking yourself?'

I have no doubt that Lindquist had mixed my drink with something that would have made me sink into a stupor. His intentions are getting clearer every day.

Tonight, I must stay awake and see what he gets up to.

20 May

It is quite early in the morning. I must try to record the peculiar experience I had last night, as a result of staying awake.

In this wooden house, no door has a threshold. Consequently, if a light is switched on in the next room, it shows through the slight gap under the door, even if it is closed. I was waiting in my room, wide awake even without having taken my special tablet to keep sleep at bay, when I heard the cuckoo clock in Lindquist's living room announce midnight. I felt certain that something important was going to happen during the night. Suddenly, I saw a crack of light under my door. Someone had switched on a light in the living room.

For a few moments, everything was quiet. Then I heard a familiar click. The light went out.

I waited a couple of minutes before padding across in my socks to my door and opening it by an inch. I peered through the gap quickly, to make sure I wasn't being watched. Then I slipped out of my room and went to the living room. Even in the dark, I could make out that the door that led to the spiral staircase was open.

I knew it would be dangerous to go down those stairs, but I was gripped by an uncontrollable scientific curiosity. I began climbing down the steps, knowing that I would have to complete three turns before I could get to the room containing the statuettes. A strange noise reached my ears as soon as I finished taking the second turn.

My ears—and all my other senses—are much sharper than most people's. Even so, it took me a long time to recognize that noise. When I did, fear and amazement froze my blood.

It was the sound of a man screaming. But his voice was far, far more sharp and shrill than a normal male voice. The language being used was Japanese.

The figure of that Japanese swimmer, Hakimoto was somehow in great peril, and was screaming loudly for help.

I just stood rooted to the spot, listening to that spine-chilling noise, when suddenly it stopped. It was then followed by a clink. The little door fixed to the cage was shut and locked. I could work that one out quite easily.

Now my curiosity rose even higher and wiped out the last traces of fear. I went down the remaining steps and peered through the open door, flattening my body against the wall.

Lindquist was unlocking the door to the cage that contained the French traveller. Then I saw him bring him out, his fist curled around the statuette. In the other hand, Lindquist was clutching something I couldn't see. But I saw him strike the figure with this unseen object. At once, Clemeau started thrashing his limbs and began a similar high-pitched wail. Lindquist showed complete indifference to what was happening. He simply ignored the screams, took out a small dropper and thrust it into Clemeau's open mouth.

Slowly, Clemeau stopped thrashing his arms and legs. Then Lindquist struck his body with the same object, and he became inert and lifeless once more. Lindquist placed the statuette upright on its feet and locked the door. I remained where I was, horrified yet mesmerised. Lindquist seemed wholly unaware of my presence.

Now it was Ackroyd's turn.

When I saw Ackroyd lying helplessly in the mad scientist's palm, I could barely contain my fury. But suddenly, Ackroyd stopped struggling. Even from that distance, it seemed as if his head was turned towards me. He screamed like the other two, but his words—though spoken with difficulty—were clear and totally unexpected. 'Shonku, what are *you* doing here? Run, run!'

As soon as he heard the little figure utter my name, Lindquist spun round as if he'd been struck by lightning. I did not wait any longer. Speeding up the stairs as quickly as I could, I ran back to my own room and locked the door.

To my complete surprise, Lindquist did not follow me.

It is now 9 a.m. No one has come to tell me that breakfast is ready. I know now that no one ever will. My door is locked from outside.

23 May

Twenty-four hours have passed since my frightful experience. Lindquist has made no attempt to see me or talk to me. There were some biscuits in my room and some fruit. I finished those, but have eaten nothing else. I am not just hungry, but also very tired. Last night, I had horrible dreams. In one, I saw a huge animal—it looked like a rat—trying to get into my room through a window. Then there was a loud explosion, followed by a bloodcurdling yell. I woke with a start, and simply lay still in my bed.

Now there is a funny smell in my room. At first, I couldn't tell where it was coming from, but now I know. It is coming through my fireplace.

And it isn't just a smell. There is smoke as well, coming through the fireplace and filling the room. I feel a little disoriented. My head is reeling, and I cannot write easily. Can't hold pen . . .

7 June

I cannot say that I am well, but isn't it a wonder that I am alive at all? I am writing my diary sitting in a Scandinavian Airways plane, bound for India. They served trout for dinner. I did not eat any of it. Perhaps I shall never be able to eat anything that I'd had in Lindquist's house.

When I am back in Giridih, I am going to think very carefully if there might be a scientific way to erase every memory of all that happened in Sulitjelma. But, in the meantime, I'd better record everything in my diary. In the future, a document describing such a horrendous event can act as a warning, if nothing else.

On 23 May, I had written about smoke seeping into my room, carrying with it a strange smell. It was that smell that made me lose consciousness. When I came round, it seemed at first as if I was lying in a huge hall. The ceiling was so high that I could hardly see it. Was I perhaps inside a church? Then, slowly, I could see the beams on the ceiling and they appeared oddly familiar.

Whatever I was lying on, felt soft under my back; but it was not a mattress on a bed for it did not remain stationary.

A little later, I stopped feeling drowsy. So I moved my head to the right to see better and, immediately, my eyes were dazzled by a bright light. Even the light did not keep still. It fell directly on my eyes at times, then moved away. When it stayed away for a while and my eyes got the chance to rest, I realized what had happened.

The light was actually being reflected from two round pieces of glass. Behind those glasses were shining two

smooth blue circles; at the centre of each blue circle was a dark dot. Those were not stationary, either. They kept darting about, occasionally stopping to stare at me. Yes, they were staring, for they were eyes. Lindquist's eyes. The glasses were his spectacles, set in a golden frame.

I was lying in the palm of his hand, which was covered by a glove. My size was now one-tenth of what it used to be. In other words, I was now a statuette, just like the others. However, I had changed only physically. I could still think and feel as before. My shoulder ached a little. Presumably, that was where I had been given an injection.

Then I could sense Lindquist bending over me,

breathing warmly over my face. His lips parted, making his gold tooth glitter. This was followed by a whiff of alcohol, more warm breath and, finally Lindquist's voice:

'What do you think of my hobby, eh, Shonku? Isn't it something unique? People collect stamps, or labels off old matchboxes, old coins, some collect autographs of famous people . . . and what do I do? I collect famous people from all over the world, turn them into statuettes, and display them in glass cases. Do you think anyone will ever give me a prize or award for this very unusual hobby, or my amazing scientific skills? No. Well, you might ask why I turned you into a little figure, when I already had a scientist in my collection. The truth is, you see, you're not here because you're a scientist, but because you are an Indian. I know I am not going to get another famous Indian so easily. How many visit Norway, anyway? In any case, not many people agree to come to my house. But you did, so here you are!'

Lindquist paused for breath. Then he licked his lips and continued, 'Do you know what my biggest triumph is? I haven't killed any of these people. I never will. Each one of them is alive. I give them an electric shock every day that makes them turn rigid and lifeless. At midnight, I give them another shock to revive them, and then I feed each one with a dropper. Sometimes, I even speak to them. But the sad thing is, although they have got absolutely nothing to worry about any more, none of them is happy. The minute I wake them up they start shrieking and yelling and beg to be rescued. Rescued! Why, I ask you? They've got such comfortable lives, food isn't a problem, no anxieties about how to earn a living . . . and yet they want to escape. I just don't understand it. But you, dear Shonku, look as if you'll be different. You'll be a good boy, won't you?'

Lindquist finished speaking. He then laid me down on the table and fastened a pair of straps across my chest and waist. I made no protest, nor struggled to free myself. I knew that would not have worked. What I needed to do was keep calm and use my brain to find a way of punishing this evil man.

According to him, an electric shock was required to turn each statuette into a lifeless object. That was not going to work on me for I was wearing a thin carbothene vest under my shirt. It was another of my inventions. A few years ago, I had gone out in a raging storm to save my saplings. While I was out in the open, a tall palm tree was struck by lightning, not far from where I was standing. I promptly lost consciousness. When I recovered, I invented carbothene—a shock resistant material—and made a vest from it, which I wear all the time.

Lindquist had moved to another part of the room. Suddenly, the light was switched off. Then I heard a wooden table being dragged, and the clinking of glass. A switch was pressed, and another bright shaft of light fell on my body. Then I saw Lindquist's glasses glitter once more. He was coming closer.

His hand came down—like the hand of a monster—clutching a thin electric wire. On his lips was an ugly smile. Then his lips parted again and his gold tooth flashed. 'Come on!' he muttered, his voice harsh and raucous, 'Come, my dear, my statuette number seven . . . come!'

His hand covered my entire body. A mild tremor that shot through my body told me that the wire had been placed on my chest. It remained there for five seconds before it was removed.

I shut my eyes and remained perfectly still, like a corpse.

The main lights were switched on again. Lindquist loosened my straps and picked me up. I held myself rigid, as if I were now just a statue.

Lindquist placed me on a table, and put a new glass lid over me. Then I heard him lock the little door. The lights went out. A few seconds later, I heard receding footsteps making their way up the spiral staircase. Then came silence.

I relaxed my limbs. The room was completely dark. I took a few steps and came across a glass wall. I tried pushing it, but it was too heavy. I sat down, leaning against the glass. The silence was broken only by the faint cries of Norwegian foxes that roamed outside. Between the glass lid and the surface of the table, there was a minuscule gap. The sound was travelling through that gap, as was a certain amount of air, which was enough to let me breathe normally.

The cuckoo clock upstairs struck three: cuckoo, cuckoo, cuckoo! Was it 3 a.m. or 3 p.m.? There was no way of telling. I began feeling a little sleepy. So I stretched my legs and tried to make myself comfortable. Now when I thought about myself, I could only laugh. I, Trilokeshwar Shonku, a world famous scientist from Bengal, recently honoured by the Swedish Academy of Science, was now a statuette, held prisoner by a crazy Norwegian.

Thoughts of my life in Giridih flashed through my mind . . . the river Usri, the Khanduli Hills, my house, Newton, Prahlad, my laboratory. The golancha tree in my garden, all my unfinished work, my research, my . . .

Tap, tap, tap!

What was that noise? A sigh was about to rise from my chest, but it stopped. I pulled my legs back and sat up straight.

Tap-tap! Tap-tap-tap! Tap-tap!

I stood up. The noise was coming from the next cage. It was Ackroyd's.

Tap-tap! Tap-tap-tap! Tap-tap!

Why, this was Morse code! Telegraphs were sent using this code. It was something I knew.

I tapped on my own glass wall this time. 'Repeat,' I said.

There were more tapping noises. Now I could make out what they meant. 'I am also wearing carbothene vest. Only pretending to be statue. Saw you the first day. Felt happy and scared, but didn't show,' said Ackroyd.

I replied, 'And the second day? When I came alone?'

'You came alone? Didn't see. Probably asleep. Practised sleeping standing up. But later . . . had to shout. To warn you.'

'How long have you been here?'

'Two years. From the time of my supposed death. Seen a lot, heard a lot, thought a lot in that time. Now there is chance to escape.'

'Escape? As a man? Or statuette?'

'Man. There is antidote. Be prepared tomorrow at

feeding time. Feel tired today. Arms feel numb. Want sleep. Good-night.'

I tapped my 'good-night' in reply. Ackroyd was alive, like me. It was I who gave him the formula for carbothene. But what 'escape' was he talking about? How was he going to do it? I had no idea. Could I become a normal man again and return to Giridih, in one piece? God knew. What did my fate hold in store for me? Who could tell?

All these thoughts kept chasing each other until I too fell asleep. When I woke, I kept sitting in the same position. The cuckoo clock continued to strike the hour. At first, I tried to keep track of time, then gave up. Then, finally, I could tell it was midnight, when I heard footsteps coming down the stairs. At once, I stood up and stiffened my arms and legs.

Lindquist opened the door and came in. He was humming under his breath. Then, with a click, he switched the lights on. I tried to see as much as I could without turning my head.

Lindquist did not come towards us. He opened another door and passed into an adjacent room. A light came on there. Now I felt bold enough to glance at Ackroyd.

Ackroyd caught my eye and smiled. Then he slowly took his hand out of his pocket. He raised it to show me what he was holding in it. It was a very small syringe, no more than an inch in length.

What he did next was even more mystifying. He replaced the syringe in his pocket and walked over to the little door of his cage. I saw him slip his little finger into the keyhole and twist it this way and that. The door opened in a few seconds. Ackroyd stepped out. I almost stopped breathing. What if Lindquist came back? Ackroyd appeared totally unconcerned. He walked over to the edge of the table, went behind the cage and glanced around a few times before springing off the table. What was he trying to do? Kill himself? No. There was an electric wire running to the ground. Ackroyd grasped it as he fell, then slowly slipped down the wire and landed on the floor quite safely. I knew he was strong and able-bodied, but had not expected to see him act like a trapeze artist.

Having reached the floor, he went to the open communicating door and stole into the next room where I had seen Lindquist disappear. By now I had become aware of a most peculiar sound that was coming from that room. It was not a human voice. What could it be? I just could not make it out.

In perhaps a couple of minutes, the noise stopped and I heard Lindquist's footsteps once more. He switched the light off in the other room and returned to mine. The first cage was quite close to the door. Lindquist took out a key, opened its door and busied himself with the Italian singer. I stood still, glancing alternately at Lindquist and at the door.

Batista—the singer—began his wail. I tried to imagine what Ackroyd might be doing in the next room. Before I could think of anything however, the door opened and Ackroyd burst into our room, magically restored to his original height and size. That six-foot-tall man then leapt forward and pounced upon Lindquist. I was imprisoned in my cage and, in any case, I did not measure any more than six inches. So there was no way I could help Ackroyd.

In just a few minutes, it became clear that Ackroyd did not require any help at all. Lindquist was naturally taken by surprise, as his attention was focused on his first statuette. By the time he could put it away safely and turn to Ackroyd, the latter had pinned him down. Then, before Lindquist could move, I saw Ackroyd take out a syringe and jab Lindquist's arm with it, in one swift, vicious movement.

And then? The next scene was more horrific, much more memorable. Only a few seconds earlier, I had seen Ackroyd attack a tall and burly man. Now I could see him clutching a six-inch long statuette in his left fist—a miniature version of Gregor Lindquist.

Ackroyd flung it aside on a table quite indifferently, and touched it once with a thin electric wire. Lindquist's body became totally inert.

Then Ackroyd walked over to me and lifted the glass lid. 'You will be able to handle such a small object far better than me,' he remarked, offering me the tiny syringe that I had seen him holding before. 'Go on, give yourself an injection!'

I asked no questions. It took only a second to inject myself. Almost at once, I regained my former height and appearance. But how did Ackroyd manage to get hold of the antidote?

When I asked him, Ackroyd simply placed a hand on my shoulder and gently steered me into the next room. Then he switched the light on.

In the middle of the room was a colossal cage made of glass, its top almost touching the ceiling. In shape it was no different from the other cages in the first room, but its occupant was not a human celebrity. It was a gigantic rodent. But it was not showing any sign of life.

Totally speechless, I could only stare at the inanimate form of the animal, then look inquiringly at Ackroyd.

'You can guess what animal that is, can't you?' asked Ackroyd. 'It is a giant version of a lemming. A real lemming is only one-tenth of this size. Lindquist was doing experiments for quite a long time—I think having produced miniatures, he now wanted to enlarge living beings. I knew he was successful in his experiments when I heard him talk about it with Hans in our room two nights ago. And that told me at once that whatever drug had been used on the lemming would work as an antidote for you and me.'

'What about all the others?' I asked, pointing at the remaining five glass cages.

Ackroyd shook his head sadly. 'They weren't wearing carbothene vests when Lindquist got hold of them. So they cannot go back to their previous forms. We'll have to treat them as dead. Come on, let's go.'

We made our way to the staircase. Ackroyd looked rather grim. I felt a sudden misgiving. 'Will you return to England?' I asked.

Ackroyd sighed. 'Did you know that services have been held in my memory? My wife wore black in mourning for several months. I believe a scholarship has been started in my name. The money comes from what I had left behind. Under these circumstances, how can I go back? It would appear most peculiar!'

'Then what will you do?'

'There is one thing that remains to be done. I haven't yet got to know the lemmings. They will soon begin their journey to the sea. I think I will join them. If a small creature like that can jump into the sea without the slightest qualm, why should I hesitate?'

12 June

I returned to Giridih four hours ago. There is just one more thing I need to record. It is related to my Norwegian experience.

As soon as I got back, Prahlad began casting curious glances at me. I was puzzled at first, but now the reason has become clear. When I tried to wear a pair of my old shoes, they felt tight. Then I tried on an old black jacket, and discovered that its sleeves were slightly shorter than before. So I measured my height, and the mystery was solved.

Instead of restoring me to my former height, Lindquist's drug has added a couple of inches to it!

Translated by Gopa Majumdar

Professor Shonku and the Box from Baghdad

19 November

Goldstein has just left for the post office to post an important letter. Let me write my diary in these few minutes I've got before he returns. He talks so much, that when he's around, there is little that one can do except listen to him. Professor Petruci is here, sitting right in front of me, but since he lost his hearing-aid in the hotel yesterday, he has been unable to hear anything. He has therefore, practically stopped trying to communicate with anyone. Luckily, he knows the local language quite well. So right now, he has got a local newspaper open in front of his face.

We are in a restaurant in Baghdad. Tables and chairs have been laid out on the pavement outside, under an awning, in the French style. We are seated at one of these tables. Coffee has been ordered; it should arrive any minute.

We came to Baghdad to attend an international inventors' conference. Scientific conferences are held frequently all over the world; but this is the first time anyone held a conference for inventors. Needless to say, my name appeared near the top of the list of invitees. No single scientist has been able to invent as many things as I. Every participant brought his latest invention. One of the main objectives of this conference, was to inform the whole world about these inventions. I brought my Omniscope, which created quite a stir in scientific circles. It looks like a pair of spectacles, and serves as a telescope, a microscope, or an x-ray machine, depending on what is required.

Yesterday was the last day of the conference. Most of the invitees who came from abroad, have gone back. The three of us have decided to spend a few more days. I had already decided, from the start, to stay an additional week after the conference. I found my two companions purely by chance.

Last night, Baghdad University hosted a dinner for the participants. On our way back to the hotel, Goldstein asked me, 'Are you leaving tomorrow?'

'No,' I replied, 'I have no wish to leave the land of Haroun Al-Rashid after just a week! I'd like to stay on for a few days and see more of this country, particularly some instances of their ancient civilization.'

Goldstein perked up at my words. 'Oh good. I'm glad to have found someone else who's staying on. But why do you mention only Haroun Al-Rashid? He was here just a thousand years ago. Think of the times before Haroun.'

'True,' I said, 'We Indians boast of our own civilization, but this one is even older. The evidence of Sumerian civilization that's been dug up by archaeologists, is 7000 years old, isn't it? Even Egypt doesn't offer anything as old as that.'

'No. You must have realized the special significance of our conference being held here? It was here in this land that people first learnt to write, 5000 years ago. That marked the beginning of our human civilization.'

Modern Iraq was once a part of what was known as Mesopotamia, situated between the Tigris and the Euphrates rivers. The very early 'civilized' people appeared around the area, now occupied by the city of Baghdad. That was the Sumerian civilization. Archaeologists have discovered samples of the oldest writings in the world, carved on stone tablets and pillars, in and around Baghdad. With great patience and perseverance, they have even deciphered the meaning behind that ancient writing.

That old civilization rose and declined many times. 4000 years ago, Semites attacked the Sumerians and defeated them. After that, history describes the rise of Babylon and Assyria. It talks of such powerful rulers as Nebuchadnezzar, Balthasar, Sennacherib and Ashurban. Some of them were kind and liberal; others were ruthless tyrants.

The tallest building in Babylon, all those years ago, measured a hundred feet. The entire city was lined with so many buildings—many of them palaces—that from a distance, it appeared to be a city of gods. Even at night it looked beautiful. Two thousand years ago, the Babylonians had already learnt to make use of the petroleum that their country possessed. They lit lamps at night with the help of this petroleum. The whole city glowed and glittered in the dark.

Eventually, Babylon was attacked by a Persian army. The Semites were crushed. Even among the Persians there were remarkable rulers—Darius, Cyrus, Xerxes. Again, some were benevolent, and others unbelievably cruel.

It was after the Persians took control in Babylon, that a nomadic Persian tribe travelled through Baluchistan and reached India. They were the Aryans. To tell the truth, the modern Irani is a descendant of the Aryans.

It is for this reason that India shares a special bond with countries in this region. There are few educated Indians who have not read the *Arabian Nights* and been moved by it. From the description in the *Arabian Nights* of Baghdad during Haroun Al-Rashid's time, it is quite clear that it was then a thriving city. The modern Baghdad may not bear a striking resemblance to it, but anyone with a little imagination will naturally think of all those tales if he finds himself in Baghdad, and feel a certain thrill.

I can see Goldstein coming back. With him is an old man I have not seen before. He seems to be a local. He is wearing a black suit, but on his head is a fez. I wonder who he is. Why is he with Goldstein?

19 November, 11 p.m.

God knows how many strange people I have met in my

sixty-five years. Such people are strewn all over the world, though I have hardly met any of them more than once. Still, I can never forget any of them.

The Iraqi I met this morning would fall into this category. It was the same man who came back with Goldstein. His name was Hasan Al-Hubbal. He was probably older than me, but his movements were quick and agile, and the look in his eyes amazingly sharp.

When Goldstein introduced him to us, he smiled and bowed. Then he took the empty chair next to me and said, 'You are the first Indian I have met. It is a great privilege for me, for I am aware of the close links between India and our country.'

I made a suitably polite reply, and was wondering why Goldstein had brought him along, when the man himself answered my unspoken question. 'I was very pleased to hear that scientists from all over the world had gathered here in Baghdad,' he said, 'I saw your pictures in the newspapers, and I wanted to meet you, but had no idea how to go about it. Today, purely by chance, I saw your friend in the post office. So I went up to him and introduced myself.'

I called the waiter and ordered another cup of coffee. Mr Al-Hubbal had settled quite comfortably in his chair, and he did not appear to be in any hurry to leave. Judging by the number of rings on his fingers and the suit he was wearing, he was a wealthy man.

He opened a gold cigarette case and extracted a black cigarette. Then he offered us each a cigarette before lighting his own.

'The question I wanted to ask you is this,' he continued, exhaling a cloud of smoke, 'You are all world famous scientists and inventors. But did you know that, in our country, a large number of things had been invented many years ago?'

'Well,' I replied, 'thanks to the archaeologists, yes, we do know about some of those things. For instance, your ancient hieroglyphics, your ancient astrology, petroleum lamps that were used 4000 years ago, your—'

Suddenly, Al-Hubbal dissolved into giggles. 'I know, I know, I know!' he said, interrupting me, 'All that is written in books; that's what the sahibs wrote. I have read it all. I know what they said. But that's nothing.'

'Nothing?' Goldstein and I cried in unison. Petruci had dropped the newspaper he was reading and was now sitting up straight, staring at Al-Hubbal's lips. Perhaps he was trying to make out the words by reading his lips.

Al-Hubbal cast his eye over the restaurant. 'This place is too crowded and noisy. If I speak softly, you won't be able to hear me, will you? Have you finished your coffee? Then let's go somewhere quiet.'

Goldstein called our waiter and paid the bill. The four of us left the restaurant and began walking towards the river.

A long paved road stretched by the Tigris, lined by palm trees. We walked in the shade, as Al-Hubbal continued to talk. 'You've read the *Arabian Nights*. haven't you?' he asked.

'Yes, of course. Who hasn't? Outside India, yours is the only country that I know of, that has such a wealth of stories. Every Indian, young or old, knows at least a handful of stories from that book,' I told him.

Al-Hubbal smiled gently. 'What do those stories tell you?'

'That a writer's imagination can be both powerful and intriguing. That it can create endless entertaining tales!'

Al-Hubbal burst into that same peculiar laughter. 'Imagination?' he asked. 'Yes, oh yes. Everyone thinks the same. So many strange tales, such weird adventures . . . of course it's all imaginary. How can any of it be real? Yet, just think. You came here to attend a conference. All of you brought your inventions, the likes of which no one had ever seen before. Some of those are extraordinary, almost unbelievable. But no one is calling them imaginary, are they? Because they are there, for all the world to see. That's why all of it is real. Isn't that right?'

Goldstein and I looked at each other without saying anything. A boat with an attractive sail was cruising down the river. It reminded me of home. 'Let's go and sit on that bench,' suggested Al-Hubbal. I looked at my watch. It was half past eleven.

Perhaps the man was slightly mad. For some time now, this idea had been bothering me. Why else did he laugh like that?

When we were seated, Al-Hubbal lit another black cigarette and said, 'If you promise not to tell a soul about the things I am going to show you, and also promise not to ask if you can have any of them . . .'

I interrupted him. 'What a strange thing to say! Why should we want any of your things?'

Al-Hubbal smiled a little dryly. 'I don't mean you, Professor Shonku, but—' he paused and glanced at

Goldstein, '—many of our valuable possessions have made their way to museums in the West. So, even if you didn't want anything for your own use, I fear you might tell some museum or other about things you've seen.'

Goldstein was looking embarrassed, but he managed to say, quite emphatically, 'No, no, why should we do that? I give you my word I would not inform any museum. But what *is* this thing that you're talking about?'

I didn't say anything, but I knew that if the object tempted Goldstein, he might covet it himself, he didn't have to inform a museum. To start with, he is an extremely wealthy American Jew. Science is no more than a pastime for him. Secondly, his true passion is antiques. In the last few days, I have seen him buy antiques in Baghdad worth nearly a thousand dollars.

Al-Hubbal spoke solemnly. 'It isn't just one thing I'm talking about. There are many, and they are scientific inventions made before the birth of Christ. We have to travel to a place seventy miles away. I will arrange transport. I have my own car.' He refused to say anything more.

Tomorrow morning, he is supposed to arrive with his car. After he left, I spoke to Goldstein and Petruci. They are both convinced that Al-Hubbal is totally crazy. One always gets to meet a few thoroughly eccentric characters virtually anywhere one goes. Al-Hubbal was obviously not mad enough to be locked up, but Goldstein and Petruci said they would not be surprised if one day, he was.

I said, 'Look at it this way. If we get to travel outside Baghdad and see more of Iraq at someone else's expense, that's not bad, is it?'

We returned to our hotel and had lunch at around half past one. Then I had a little rest. The climate here is very good. I feel quite refreshed and invigorated.

20 November

It is hardly surprising that we should have a wondrous experience in a wonderful city like Baghdad. But what happened today was well beyond my expectations. Fairy tales belong to an imaginary world. Reading them, or hearing them, may give us a special joy. But if several things from fairy tales suddenly appear in real life, it is easy to feel confused.

Let me explain what happened today.

True to his word, Hasan Al-Hubbal turned up in his green Citroen on the dot of eight-thirty. In the car was a basket. He gave us that odd smile again. 'That basket contains your lunch,' he informed us, 'You are my guests for the whole day.'

We left by nine o'clock. Petruci had enquired in various places yesterday, and managed to find a new hearing-aid. Today, his whole demeanour had changed. Goldstein appeared to be a fun-loving person, in any case. As we were getting in the car, he said, 'When I was a child, we used to go for picnics in large numbers. This is another picnic!'

Then he winked at me. I could tell that Goldstein had not believed a single word Al-Hubbal had said. If he had agreed to come with us, it was only because he had nothing better to do. He was certainly not expecting anything more than just a pleasant outing.

We crossed a bridge over the Tigris and went

westward. There weren't many trees here, it looked more like a desert. However, as it was the month of November, it wasn't hot at all.

'The spot where I'm taking you,' said Al-Hubbal as he drove, 'is situated at a place where the Tigris and the Euphrates are separated by only twenty-five miles. One reason why Babylon made such a lot of progress was because these rivers were so close.'

A question had been hovering in my mind since yesterday. Now I couldn't help asking it. 'Are you a scientist? I mean, an archaeologist or something like that?'

Al-Hubbal replied, 'If by a scientist, you mean someone with a degree in science, then no, I am not a scientist. And if by an archaeologist you mean someone who digs in the earth to discover evidence of ancient civilizations, then yes, I am certainly an archaeologist.'

By this time, we had left the plains and were driving uphill. In the distance was a range of hills. 'Those hills mark the border of Iraq. Beyond them is Persia,' explained Al-Hubbal.

The scenery outside had started to change. Within a few minutes, we entered a mountain pass, making our way through high, steep hills. Before travelling to Baghdad, I had done some reading about the place. Now I asked, 'Are we in the Abu Quiab region?' Al-Hubbal said, 'Yes, that's right. Our destination is just ten miles from here.'

Sunlight did not reach the pass easily, so it felt quite cool. I wrapped my scarf more securely round my neck. Petruci had not said a single word since we started. It was very difficult to make him out. I looked at Goldstein.

He seemed to have nodded off.

As soon as we emerged from the pass, the landscape changed again. I saw greenery in the distance, which could only mean that there was no dearth of trees on this side. Here and there, rising through the treetops, were grey hillocks.

Our car took a left turn from the main road. Al-Hubbal was humming an Iraqi song—it sounded like Indian music. How old would Al-Hubbal be? It was impossible to guess. When he smiled, endless lines appeared near his eyes. He might be very old, perhaps ninety or thereabouts. Yet how energetic he was! He'd been driving at a speed of sixty miles since leaving Baghdad, but was not showing the slightest sign of fatigue.

Ten minutes later, the car stopped by a juniper tree. 'We have to walk the remaining way,' said Al-Hubbal, 'It's only a quarter of a mile from here.'

We got out of the car and began walking. It was very still and very quiet outside, with not a soul in sight. There were plenty of trees—willow, oak, juniper, date palms. Birds were calling out occasionally. I heard a bulbul and immediately thought of home. At places, sunlight was streaming through the leaves. Its warmth felt most pleasant.

Then we came upon a very big rocky mound. It was spread over a large area and was as tall as a four-storeyed building. We were walking by the side of this mound when, suddenly, Al-Hubbal said, 'Here we are!'

Where were we? To our right rose the mound, to our left was a wood. There was nothing else to be seen. What was so special about this place?

I looked at Al-Hubbal. His face looked transformed. His eyes were glinting; there was an air of suppressed excitement about him. He couldn't keep his hands still. Suddenly, he gave another of his giggles, ran his eyes over all three of us, and spoke in a low voice, 'You are inventors, aren't you? Well-known scientists of the twentieth century? Very well then, see now what the scientists in the first century had achieved. Open sesame!'

To be honest, he didn't actually say 'open sesame'. In fact, he used the Arabic word 'Sim Sim!' But the effect that word produced was perfectly incredible.

A huge boulder, lying loose on a corner of the mound, began moving to one side, making a low rumbling noise. Then it stopped, and we could only gape at the dark tunnel it exposed.

For a few moments, Al-Hubbal allowed himself to enjoy our open-mouthed amazement. Then he bowed, pointed—somewhat dramatically—at the tunnel, and said, 'Welcome to Ali Baba's cave!'

We followed Al-Hubbal into the dark passage. When we were all in, he shouted, 'Close sesame!' At once, the boulder rumbled back into place, neatly closing the 'gate'. We were engulfed by impenetrable darkness. What was Al-Hubbal up to? The whole thing smacked of a carefully calculated plot. I didn't like it at all.

Then we heard the sound of a match being struck. In the next instant, the cave was filled with a pale yellow light. Al-Hubbal had lit a lamp. In that light, when I looked around, I saw that a scene that had existed only in my imagination when I was a child, had presented itself here, in real life. The place where we were

standing could only be described as Ali Baba's cave. Shelves had been made on the stone walls, and niches carved, to store an endless variety of objects. There were boxes, cases, chests, bowls, pots, pitchers, vases and chairs. All were made of metal—some might have been made of gold—and all were studded with bright, sparkling gems. Helped by the light from the lamp, they suffused the entire cave with a colourful glow.

At first, we were rendered speechless. Each of us simply stared at this fantastic sight. Then Goldstein found his tongue. 'What do you think you're doing? You think we are foolish little boys? Do you seriously think you can play a trick on three scientists and get away with it?' he cried in his deep voice.

Strangely enough, these harsh words did not seem to cause Al-Hubbal any offence. In the flickering light of the lamp, I saw him looking at Goldstein with a smile on his lips, shaking his head gently. Then he asked, 'Can any of you read the Sumerian script, written 5000 years ago?'

'Yes, I can,' replied Petruci quickly, 'I was an archaeologist. Twelve years ago I had severe heat stroke while working in Iran. It nearly killed me. After that, I gave up digging. But why do you ask?'

Al-Hubbal took the lamp over to another corner of the cave. A stone slab—about five feet in length and three feet wide—was standing upright. On it were carved various letters and characters. 'See if you can read this!' invited Al-Hubbal.

Petruci knelt down on the floor, took the lamp from Al-Hubbal and leant over the stone to read the writing on it. For a few moments, his lips moved, and he simply muttered to himself. Ten minutes later, he rose to his feet and said, 'Where did you find this? This stone slab cannot possibly belong here!'

'First tell me what that writing says,' implored Al-Hubbal.

'It describes this cave, and gives its location. It also mentions the secret code that will open and close the gate. And it says that the supreme magician, Gemal Nishahir, is buried in this cave, together with an amazing casket made by him.'

'Doesn't it say anything else?' Now there was a note of excitement in Al-Hubbal's quiet voice.

'Yes, there is more.'

'Well?'

'It says that the casket will act like living history. Anyone who refuses to believe this history, or treats the casket with disrespect, will bring upon himself the curse of a god—the god in the temple, on top of the ziggurat.'

Al-Hubbal nodded gravely and said, 'Hm'.

Goldstein shouted again, 'Open that gate. We should not spend long in here—the air in this cave is polluted, harmful.'

This struck me as an exaggeration. Al-Hubbal did not pay him the slightest attention. Petruci said, 'It seems to me that this stone has come from the Kish region. But I am very curious to know how you found it.'

Al-Hubbal's reply astonished me. He spoke calmly, without betraying any sign of either anxiety or agitation. 'Seven years ago,' he said, 'Sir John Hollingworth came to the Kish region to excavate. I am sure all of you are aware of that. I was in his team as the official interpreter. When this slab of stone was found, I managed to read the writing secretly, before Sir John. The next day, I simply disappeared with it. I did not see anything wrong in doing that. Even now, I believe what I did was right, for it belonged to our own country. If I had let Sir John keep it, do you think it would have remained in Baghdad? No. It would have gone either to the British

Museum, or to some other museum in the West. I, on the other hand, have kept it where it belonged, and in a place where it cannot be damaged.'

Goldstein was sitting on a small boulder. Now he sprang up, driven to the very edge of his patience. 'You are a criminal!' he yelled. 'Fraud! Cheat! I don't know about the writing or that stone slab, or all the other stuff, but do you want us to believe that your technique to open that gate is a five-thousand-year-old scientific method? You mean modern science hasn't played any role in it? There aren't electrical gadgets hidden in cracks and crannies in these rocks?'

Al-Hubbal raised his right hand to calm Goldstein down. 'The way you are shouting, sir, I fear you might wake the person who has been resting here as a skeleton for fifty centuries. I beg of you, Dr Goldstein, do not get so worked up!'

Goldstein stopped short, looked a little confused and said, 'Skeleton?'

Al-Hubbal picked up the lamp again and moved behind the stone slab. We followed him, and realized that the cave spread out here and became more square in shape, like a courtyard. In the middle of it was a deep, dark hole. Al-Hubbal lowered the lamp so that its light fell into the hole. We saw a skeleton, lying on its back, surrounded by a few old pots made of terracotta.

Al-Hubbal stretched a hand towards the skeleton and said, 'That's the master magician, Gemal Nishahir Al-Hararit!'

Even in that dim light, I could see beads of perspiration on Goldstein's forehead. He pulled a face and said, 'I fail to see why we should have to put up with such a horrible joke. Will you open the gate or not?'

Al-Hubbal did not reply. All he did was shift his calm gaze from the skeleton and rest it on Goldstein.

Goldstein decided to take matters into his own hands. Without waiting for Al-Hubbal to speak, he shouted, 'Sim Sim!'

We stared at the gate for a few seconds, in absolute silence. Nothing happened. The gate remained closed. This time, shaking with rage, Goldstein pounced upon Al-Hubbal and grabbed him by his collar. 'Will you open that gate this instant, or not?'

Petruci and I pulled him back. Al-Hubbal finally opened his mouth, sounding serious once more. 'Dr Goldstein, you are getting worked up over nothing. That code has to be uttered in a certain tone, at a certain pitch. Only I know what is required, you don't. When I located this cave, I had to practise uttering that code for twenty days before I got it right. So—'

Goldstein interrupted him impatiently, 'All right, all right. *You* say it then. I can't bear to be in this stuffy, airless space!'

'But,' said Al-Hubbal, 'how can I open the gate without telling you the real reason why I brought you here? What if you don't grant me my request?'

'What request?' we cried.

Al-Hubbal picked up the lamp and walked over to the centre of the cave. The light fell on a mound. On top of that mound was a strange looking casket. It appeared to be made of copper, but was inlaid with gold and silver. And, once again, there were precious stones of various colours and different sizes set in it.

Although I am calling it a casket, there didn't seem to be a lid, or anything that could be removed to open it.

'What is this?' asked Goldstein.

'Is this the box that the stone slab mentions?' said Petruci.

'Yes, what else could it be?' Al-Hubbal replied. 'When I first discovered this cave, there was nothing in it except that skeleton and this box.'

'But,' I said, 'that writing speaks of some living history preserved in this box. What does that mean?'

Al-Hubbal smiled a little wanly. 'That is the biggest puzzle,' he said. 'I have not been able to work it out, although God knows I have tried. Now do you understand why I brought you here?'

We exchanged glances. Then Goldstein spoke again. 'You want us to solve this mystery?'

'Yes,' said Al-Hubbal, 'but I can hardly force you to agree. I can only make a request.'

'Count me out of this!' said Goldstein clearly, 'I believe that box is empty.'

Goldstein picked it up. Al-Hubbal did not stop him. All he said, speaking under his breath, was, 'If you do not treat it with respect, the god on top of the ziggurat will be displeased!'

Goldstein put the box back with an air of indifference. Now I picked it up. Petruci stood by my side. Al-Hubbal came closer with the lamp in his hand.

The box felt quite heavy. I shook it and felt something gentle rattle inside.

'We cannot solve any mystery standing here in this cave,' I said. 'Will you please let us take it back to the hotel, just for a day? It will be treated with every respect,

I promise you.'

Al-Hubbal stared at me for a few seconds. Then he said, 'Do you believe in the supernatural powers of the ancient gods?'

'I have a very deep respect for everything that belongs to our past, especially if it is as beautiful as this casket.'

Al-Hubbal smiled. 'Very well, I believe you.'

So saying, he moved away and walked back to the gate. Then he stood very close to the wall and shouted again, using the same funny sing-song tone: 'Sim Sim!'

Immediately, the wall slid back and daylight poured in through the gap. We emerged from the cave at last, and heaved sighs of relief.

Al-Hubbal then invited us to help ourselves to the contents of the lunch basket. It turned out to be filled with bread, cheese, delicious sweets and fruit.

By the time we arrived at the hotel with the box, it was almost 7 p.m. Goldstein was still grumbling. He was most annoyed that we had treated Al-Hubbal in a friendly fashion and agreed to examine the box. Once we were inside the hotel, he turned to Al-Hubbal and said, 'If this turns out to be a hoax, I will report you immediately to the police. You yourself have admitted to theft. So it shouldn't be difficult to have you suitably punished. Just remember that.'

Al-Hubbal smiled. 'I am eighty-two. What punishment can you possibly give me now? I have only one wish left in life—to find out what mystery lies in that box. Once I've learnt that, it will make no difference to me whether I live or die, or whether I am punished or not.'

Then he turned to me. 'You will find it difficult to contact me as I do not have a telephone. I will return here myself, some time tomorrow morning.' With these words, he bowed to each of us, and then went out through the front door to disappear into the dark night.

*

It is now half past ten. Petruci and I have spent the last two hours trying to unravel Al-Hubbal's 'mystery'. All we have succeeded in doing is identifying a particular stone fixed on the box—a large carnelian—that can be unscrewed. We managed to take it out and discovered that, behind it, was a small container. It looked black. I smelt it and realized that something like wax or paraffin had been used on it, which had made it turn dark. I wanted to light a wick and hold it over the container. But neither of us had any paraffin, nor was it possible to get it at this late hour. So we decided to wait till tomorrow morning before having another go.

Goldstein did not come to my room even once. I rang him in his. He said he wasn't feeling well. He had an aching head and cramps in his stomach. If the god in the temple really has any supernatural power, perhaps he has already started cursing Goldstein, thereby causing him so much discomfort. Who knows?

21 November, 6.30 a.m.

Let me record the extraordinary occurrence that I witnessed a short while ago.

I am an early riser. This morning, I rose earlier than usual, possibly because I had a certain amount of anxiety on my mind. By the time I had had a shower and a cup of coffee, dawn had broken. There were white, fluffy clouds scattered all over the sky. I looked at the colours of dawn play upon these, and thought of the cave from the *Arabian Nights.* That reminded me of the phrase 'sim sim'. Almost unconsciously, I happened to say it aloud, not once, but two or three times. I realized what I'd done, only when a sudden click made me turn around.

The mysterious box was placed on a bedside table. Now when I looked at it, I saw that a lapis lazuli—as big as a 50 paisa coin—had slid out of the surface of the box, and was hanging open like a door, still held to the box with the help of a tiny hinge. Amazingly, the code for opening the box was the same as the gate to the cave; only the tone used was required to be slightly different.

I peered through the open 'door'. The inside of the box was packed with tiny gadgets. These were made of not just metal, but what appeared to be pieces of glass and beads. It was impossible to tell what those gadgets were meant to do, since I had never seen anything like them before. I tried using my own Omniscope to examine them more closely, but even that did not help.

Then I lifted the box from the table and took it closer to the window. For the first time, I could see it clearly in broad daylight. Opposite the carnelian, was a little hole. I used my omniscope again to peer through that hole. There was another stone fixed on the other side. Could it be a diamond? Yes, that's what it looked like. But why was it placed there? Its purpose was not clear.

What we have to do now is light that container inside the box. That will act as a lamp. Petruci has offered to look for paraffin as soon as the shops open.

I have handled a lot of complex machinery in my life, but nothing as perplexing as this.

22 November, 8 p.m.

Bravo Haroun Al-Rashid! Bravo Sumerian civilization! Kudos to ancient scientists! Gemal Nishahir Al-Hararit—I salute you!

There is only one reason for such jubilation. We have found evidence of such a brilliant scientific mind that our own achievements have paled into insignificance. I have decided to throw my Omniscope into the Tigris. How I'll find the enthusiasm to work again when I go back home, I do not know. Never before have I experienced such an odd mixture of joy, wonder, despair, excitement and fear.

Yesterday morning, Al-Hubbal rang me from somewhere, barely half an hour after I finished writing my diary. 'How is it going? Have you got anywhere?' he asked.

When I explained about the strange occurrence earlier, he became very excited. 'I am coming over to your hotel at once! And I will bring some paraffin. Tell Petruci not to bother.'

The three of us in the hotel had our breakfast together. Goldstein looked ill. All he had was a cup of coffee. 'I didn't sleep very well last night,' he said, 'Even when I did get a few minutes' sleep, I had awful nightmares!'

At this, Petruci started making some light-hearted remark about the curse of the god. Goldstein interrupted him, looking most annoyed, and said, 'If you believe in such superstitions, you do not deserve to be called a scientist. The reason why I am feeling unwell, is simply that I was cooped up in that stupid cave yesterday for so long! There cannot possibly be any other reason.'

However, when Al-Hubbal turned up a little later, carrying some paraffin, Goldstein decided to join us, perhaps because he had nothing else to do. I saw him come into my room and flop down on a sofa. Al-Hubbal and Petruci were already there. I shut the door, so that we were not disturbed by unexpected callers. Then I got to work.

The first thing I did was to unscrew the carnelian, take out the container from the box, and fill it with paraffin. Then I tore my handkerchief and rolled a strip of cloth into a wick, which I dipped in the paraffin. Then I lit one end of it. Goldstein was sitting opposite me. As soon as I placed the burning wick in the container, a light appeared from somewhere and fell on Goldstein's clothes. How could that happen?

For a few moments, I was totally taken aback. Then I remembered the little diamond that I had seen earlier, fixed at one end of the box. Clearly, that stone was acting as a lens. As soon as the container became a lamp, its light passed through that transparent lens and fell on Goldstein.

I looked at Al-Hubbal. His eyes were lit up with wonder. Goldstein was looking uncomfortable. He got up and moved to one side. Al-Hubbal ran and pushed the empty sofa out of the way. That exposed the wall behind it, and the light naturally fell on the wall. I realized the shape of the light was circular, as if it was a beam shining out of a torch.

Petruci shouted in his mother tongue: '*La lanterna magica*!'

A magic lantern? But where were the pictures?

I looked at the box again. The 'door' that had opened upon hearing the words 'sim sim' was still hanging open. I inserted my index finger through the little gap and, very cautiously, felt the tiny gadgets fitted inside. Soon, my finger came to rest upon an object that felt like the point of a pencil. I pressed it gently. What followed took my breath away.

The moment I pressed that sharp object, something inside the box began whirring. The light on the wall no longer appeared stationary. It was trembling and, only a second later, various images began to appear on the wall.

Petruci went quickly over to the window and shut it. Now my room was totally dark. There was no light except what was coming from the box.

And the wall? In speechless wonder, we saw moving images on it. They were slightly hazy, but it was easy enough to see what they meant to convey. It was exactly like watching a modern film, except that the area on which the pictures fell was circular in shape, not rectangular.

But what *was* being shown? Which city was this? Who were these people? Why were there so many of them? Was it a festival of some kind?

Petruci shouted again, 'A funeral! It is a funeral procession. Someone famous must have died. Look, there's the coffin.'

Yes, a coffin was being carried. How many people were following it? Ten thousand? They were wearing strange clothes, their hair was arranged in a flamboyant style. I noticed that many of them were holding fans with patterns and designs on them, and waving them together. Then there were vehicles with four wheels, being drawn by animals that looked like cows.

'I know!' said Petruci, 'It's Ur! A king in ancient Ur must have died. When a king died there, sixty or seventy others took poison to die with their king. They were all buried together.'

I could not bear to watch any more. My head began reeling. I moved away to sit on my bed. This four-thousand-year-old cinema had totally overpowered my brain.

I do not know how long the film ran. Suddenly, I saw that the window had been thrown open once more, and Al-Hubbal was in the process of blowing out the lamp in the box. His face suggested that he had no idea what he should say or do. The three scientists in the room were equally overwhelmed. None of us could speak.

It was Al-Hubbal who finally broke the silence. He folded his hands and bowed to all of us. 'I cannot thank you enough,' he said. 'You have helped me fulfil my last desire, and I am extremely grateful that I could show you just how extraordinary our ancient civilization was. But remember one thing. You must not tell anyone about this box. If you do, no one is going to believe you, anyway. Dr Goldstein called me a fraud. People will call you insane. You could never prove your claim because this box will now go back where it belongs. That has been its home for the last 4000 years, that is where it will always remain. I will now take my leave. *Khuda hafiz*!'

Al-Hubbal had brought with him the same basket in which he'd packed our lunch yesterday. He placed the box in it and walked out.

The three of us sat in silence for a few minutes, feeling a little foolish. Then Petruci turned to Goldstein and asked, 'Do you still think he is a cheat?'

Goldstein seemed to have recovered. His eyes were gleaming with some new idea. Instead of answering Petruci's question, he rose and began pacing restlessly. Then he suddenly turned to me and said, 'Such a wonderful object is going to remain hidden in a cave for ever? No, that cannot be!'

I did not like these words. 'So many wonderful and extraordinary objects from our ancient past may still be hidden and buried under the earth,' I replied. 'Nobody has seen them. No one knows they are there. That box could be one of them. Forget all that you saw, pretend it didn't happen.'

'Impossible!' Goldstein roared. 'That man is a thief, there is no question about that. He has no right to keep that box. I want it, and I am going to get it. No matter how much it costs. God knows I have plenty of money!'

Before either Petruci or I could stop him, Goldstein rushed out of the room like a hurricane. Petruci shook his head. 'It's a mistake . . . I think Goldstein is making a terrible mistake. Shonku, I don't like this at all,' he muttered.

After pacing up and down the length of my room

for a few minutes, Petruci returned to his own. I continued to sit on my bed, still thinking of those scenes from the funeral procession of a king of Ur who died 4000 years ago. Until today, it had never been brought home to me how far our ancient predecessors had progressed in science and technology.

Petruci rang me in the evening with the news that Goldstein had not returned. I rang Goldstein's room half an hour ago. There was no reply. It is quite late now. There is nothing that we can do before tomorrow. I can't help thinking of the divine curse. What has Goldstein let himself in for?

23 November

I could not have dreamt that our astounding experience in Baghdad would end like this. What we did see was what greed can do to a man. My only comfort is that I managed to intervene in the nick of time, thus avoiding an even more tragic ending.

I rang Goldstein early in the morning. There was still no reply. Then I spoke to Petruci, and we agreed that we would have to investigate the matter. It had occurred to both of us that we would have to go back to that cave. Al-Hubbal had gone there. When Goldstein rushed out, it must have been to chase Al-Hubbal.

Our hotel manager, Mr Farouki, arranged a car for us as soon as we told him we wanted to sightsee. Petruci and I left for the cave at half past six.

It took us an hour and a half to cover seventy miles. We asked our driver to stop the car where Al-Hubbal had stopped his. Then we told him to wait for us, and set off on foot to look for the cave.

We found the hillock easily enough, but the gate to the cave was closed. This was only to be expected, of course, but Petruci appeared thoroughly dismayed. 'Oh no, we simply wasted our time!' he exclaimed. 'I don't think there's anything to be done, except perhaps blow it up with dynamite.'

'Before we do that,' I offered, 'let me test my memory.'

'Your memory? You mean you can say that code exactly like Al-Hubbal? In that same tone?' Petruci sounded perfectly incredulous.

In reply, I simply cupped my hands around my mouth. Then I raised my voice a few notches, and shouted, 'Sim Sim!'

Nothing happened for a few moments. Then a rumble started, sounding like distant thunder. A lizard, suddenly frightened, scuttled across the grass and disappeared. Slowly, the gate to the cave slid back, exposing the dark emptiness within. Petruci and I entered it with trembling hearts.

We were both carrying torches. When we switched them on, all we could see at first were the sparkling stones and gems on those various objects piled high on the shelves. Then we found the mound on which the magic box had been resting. Both of us shone our torches on it. The box was gone. There was no sign of it.

Petruci walked on towards the far corner. Suddenly I heard him gasp. So I ran across to join him.

Petruci's torch was shining on something lying on the floor. It was Goldstein. He was lying flat on his back. His eyes were open.

I shone my own torch on the same spot. It lit up the whole corner. What we saw then froze our blood. Only a few feet away from Goldstein, also lying flat on his back, was Al-Hubbal. His arms were wrapped around the casket that contained a four-thousand-year-old film. Next to Al-Hubbal was the skeleton of Gemal Nishahir. It was lying there exactly as we had seen it before.

I felt Goldstein's pulse and heaved a sigh of relief. It was weak, but still beating. If we could take him out of the cave immediately and get a doctor, perhaps his life could be saved.

But Al-Hubbal? His life had come to an end. It seemed likely that he had died the day before, because when I tried to loosen the box from his grasp, it proved quite impossible. His cold, stiff arms had imprisoned that casket for ever.

*

We returned to the hotel with Goldstein about an hour ago. He has regained consciousness. A doctor has examined him, and told us that there is nothing wrong with him physically. However, it is clear to Petruci and I, that a major change has come over Goldstein, because when we asked him what happened last night, he simply grinned inanely and said, 'Sim Sim!'

Since then, he has been asked innumerable questions. For every question, he has only one answer. 'Sim Sim!' he says, giving the same foolish smile.

Translated by Gopa Majumdar

CORVUS

15 August

Birds have fascinated me for a long time. When I was a boy, we had a pet mynah which we taught to pronounce clearly more than a hundred Bengali words. I knew of course, that although some birds could talk, they didn't understand the meaning of what they said. But one day our mynah did something so extraordinary that I was forced to revise my opinion. I had just got back from school, Mother had brought me a plate of halwa, when the mynah suddenly screeched, 'Earthquake! Earthquake!' We had felt nothing but next day the papers reported that a slight tremor had indeed been recorded by the seismograph.

Ever since then, I have felt a curiosity about the intelligence of birds, although in my preoccupation with various scientific projects, I have not been able to pursue it in any way. My cat, Newton, contributed to this neglect. Newton doesn't like birds, and I don't wish to do anything that would displease him. Lately, however—perhaps because of age—Newton has grown increasingly indifferent to birds. Which is probably why my laboratory is being regularly visited by crows, sparrows and other common birds. I feed them in the morning, and in anticipation of this, they begin to clamour outside my window from well before sunrise.

Every creature is born with skills peculiar to its species. I believe such skills are more pronounced and more startling in birds than in other creatures. Examine a weaver-bird's nest, and it will make you gasp with astonishment. Given the ingredients to construct such a nest, a man would either throw up his hands in despair or take months of ceaseless effort to do so.

There is a species of birds in Australia called the Malle Fowl which builds its nest on the ground. Sand, earth and vegetable matter go into the making of this hollow mound which is provided with a hole for entry. The bird lays its eggs inside the mound but doesn't sit on them to hatch. Yet without heat the eggs won't hatch, so what is the answer? Simply this: by some amazing and as yet unknown process, the Malle Fowl maintains a constant temperature of seventy-eight degrees Fahrenheit inside the mound, regardless of whether it is hot or cold outside.

Nobody knows why a bird called the Grebe, should pluck out its feathers to eat them and feed its young with them. The same Grebe while floating in water can, by some unknown means, reduce its own specific gravity at the sight of a predator so that it floats with only its head above the water.

We all know of the amazing sense of direction of migratory birds, the prowess of eagles and falcons, the vultures' keen sense of smell, and the enchanting gift of singing possessed by numerous birds. It is for this reason that I have been wanting for some time to devote a little more time to the study of birds. How much can a bird be taught beyond its innate skills? Is it possible to instil human knowledge and intelligence in one? Can a machine be constructed to do this?

20 September

1 believe in the simple method, so my machine will be a simple one. It will consist of two sections: one will be a cage to house the bird; the other will transmit intelligence to the bird's brain by means of electrodes.

For the past month I have been carefully studying the birds which come into my laboratory for food. Apart from the ubiquitous crows and sparrows, birds such as pigeons, doves, parakeets and bulbuls also come. Amongst all these, one particular bird has caught my attention: a crow. Not the jet black raven, but the ordinary crow. I can easily make him out from the other crows. Apart from the tiny white spot below the right eye which makes him easily recognizable, his behaviour too, marks him out from other crows. For instance, I have never seen a crow hold a pencil in its beak and make marks on the table with it. Yesterday he did something which really surprised me. I was working on my machine when I heard a soft rasping noise. I turned round and saw that the crow had taken a matchstick from a half-open matchbox, and holding it in his beak, was scraping it against the side of the box.

When I shooed him away, he flew across, sat on the window and proceeded to utter some staccato sounds which bore no resemblance to the normal cawing of a crow. In fact, for a minute I thought the crow was laughing!

27 September

I finished assembling my Ornithon machine today. The crow has been in the lab since morning, eating breadcrumbs and hopping from window to window. As soon as I placed the cage on the table and opened the door, the crow flew over and hopped inside, a sure sign that he is extremely eager to learn. Since a familiarity with language is essential for the bird to follow my instructions, I have started with simple Bengali lessons. All the lessons being pre-recorded, all I have to do is press buttons. Different lessons are in different channels, and each channel bears a different number. I have noticed a strange thing; as soon as I press a button the crow's eyes close and his movements cease. For a bird as restless as a crow, this is unusual indeed.

A conference of ornithologists is being held in November in Santiago, the capital of Chile. I have written to my ornithologist friend Rufus Grenfell in Minnesota. If my feathered friend is able to acquire some human intelligence, I should like to take him to the conference for a lecture-demonstration.

4 October

Corvus is the Latin name for the genus crow. I have started calling my pupil by that name. In the beginning, he used to answer my call by a turn of the head in my direction. Now he responds vocally. For the first time I heard a crow saying 'ki' (what?) instead of 'caw'. But I don't expect speech will ever be his forte. Corvus will never turn into a talking crow. Whatever intelligence he acquires, will show in his actions.

Corvus is learning English now; if I do go abroad for a demonstration, English would help. Lessons last an hour between eight and nine in the morning. The rest of the day he hangs around the lab. In the evening, he still prefers to go back to the mango tree in the north-east corner of my garden.

Newton seems to have accepted Corvus. After what happened today, I shouldn't be surprised if they end up as friends. It happened in the afternoon. Corvus for once, was away somewhere, I was sitting in the armchair scribbling in my notebook, and Newton was curled up on the floor alongside when a flapping sound made me turn towards the window. It was Corvus. He had just come in with a freshly cut piece of fish in his beak. He dropped it in front of Newton, went back to the window, and sat surveying the scene with little twists of his neck.

Grenfell has replied to my letter. He says he is arranging to have me invited to the ornithologists' conference.

20 October

Unexpected progress in the last two weeks. With a pencil held in his beak, Corvus is now writing English words and numerals.

The paper is placed on the table, and Corvus writes standing on it. He wrote his own name in capital letters:

C-O-R-V-U-S. He can do simple addition and subtraction, write down the capital of England when asked to, and can even write my name. Three days ago I taught him the months, days and dates. When asked what day of the week it was today, he wrote in clear letters:

F-R-I-D-A-Y.

That Corvus is clever in his eating habits too, was proved today. I had kept some pieces of toast on one plate and some guava jelly on another in front of him; each time he put a piece in his mouth, he smeared some jelly on it first with his beak.

22 October

I had clear proof today that Corvus now wants to stay away from other crows. There was a heavy shower, and after an ear-splitting thunderclap I looked out of the window and saw the simul tree outside my garden smouldering. In the afternoon, after the rain stopped, there was a tremendous hue and cry set up by the neighbourhood crows who had all gathered around the simul tree. I sent my servant Prahlad to investigate. He came back and said, 'Sir, there's a dead crow lying at the foot of the tree; that's why there is such excitement.' I realized the crow had been struck by lightning. But strangely enough, Corvus didn't leave my room at all. He held a pencil in his beak and was absorbed in writing the prime numbers: 1, 2, 3, 5, 7, 11, 13 . . .

7 November

Corvus can now be proudly displayed in scientific

circles. Birds can be taught to do small things, but a bird as intelligent and educated as Corvus, is unique in history. The Ornithon has done its job well. Questions which can be answered in a few words, or with the help of numbers, on subjects as diverse as mathematics, history, geography and the natural sciences, Corvus is now able to answer. Along with that, Corvus has spontaneously acquired what can only be termed human intelligence, something which has never been associated with birds. I shall give an example. I was packing my suitcase this morning in preparation for my trip to Santiago. As I finished and closed the lid, I found Corvus standing by with the key in his beak.

Another letter from Grenfell yesterday. He is already in Santiago. The organizers of the conference are looking forward to my visit. Till now these conferences have only dealt with birds in the abstract; never has a live bird been used in a demonstration. The paper I have written, is based on the priceless knowledge I have gathered in the last two months about bird behaviour. Corvus will be there in person to silence my critics.

10 November

I'm writing this on the plane to South America. I have only one incident to relate. As we were about to leave the house, I found Corvus greatly agitated and obviously anxious to get out of the cage. I couldn't make out the reason for this; nevertheless, I opened the cage door. Corvus hopped out, flew over to my desk and started pecking furiously at the drawer. I opened it and found my passport still lying in it.

I have had a new kind of cage built for Corvus. It maintains the temperature that best suits the bird. For his food, I have prepared tiny globules which are both tasty and nutritious. Corvus has aroused everyone's curiosity on the plane as they have probably never seen a pet crow before. I haven't told anyone about the uniqueness of my pet—I prefer to keep it secret. Corvus too, probably sensing this, is behaving like any ordinary crow.

14 November

Hotel Excelsior, Santiago, 11 p.m. I have been too busy these last couple of days to write. Let me first describe what happened at the lecture, then I shall come to the disconcerting events of a little while ago. To cut a long story short, my lecture has been another feather in my cap. My paper took half an hour to read; then followed an hour's demonstration with the crow. I had released Corvus from the cage and put him down on the table as soon as I ascended the podium. It was a long mahogany table behind which sat the organizers of the conference, while I stood to one side speaking into the microphone. As long as I spoke, Corvus listened with the utmost attention, with occasional nods to suggest that he was getting the drift of my talk. To the applause that followed my speech, Corvus made his own contribution by beating a tattoo with his beak on the surface of the table.

The demonstration that followed, gave Corvus no respite. All that he had learnt in the past two months, he now demonstrated to the utter amazement of the delegates, who all agreed that they had never imagined a bird could be capable of such intelligent behaviour.

The evening edition of the local newspaper *Correro de Santiago* splashed the news on the front page with a picture of Corvus holding a pencil in his beak.

After the meeting, Grenfell and I went on a sight-seeing tour of Santiago with the chairman Signor Covarrubias. It is a bustling, elegant metropolis, to the east of which the Andes range stands like a wall between Chile and Argentina. After an hour's drive Covarrubias turned to me and said, 'You must have noticed in our programme that we have made various arrangements for the entertainment of our delegates. I should particularly like to recommend the show this evening by the Chilean magician Argus. His speciality is that he uses a lot of trained birds in his act.'

I was intrigued, so Grenfell and I went to the Plaza theatre to watch Señor Argus. It is true that he uses a lot of birds. Ducks, parrots, pigeons, hens, a four-foot-high crane, a flock of humming birds—all these Argus deploys with much evidence of careful training. But none of these birds comes anywhere near Corvus. Frankly, I found the magician himself far more interesting than his birds. Over six feet tall, he has a parrot-like nose, and his hair, parted in the middle, is as slick and shiny as a new gramophone record. He wears spectacles so high-powered that they turn his pupils into a pair of tiny black dots, and out of the sleeves of his jet-black coat emerges a pair of hands whose pale, tapering fingers cast a spell on the audience with their sinuous movements. Not that the conjuring was of a high order, but the conjuror's presence and personality were well worth the price of admission. As I came out of the theatre, I remarked to Grenfell that it wouldn't be a bad idea to show Señor Argus some of Corvus's tricks, now that he had shown us his.

Dinner was followed by excellent Chilean coffee and a stroll in the hotel garden with Grenfell. It was past ten when I returned to my room. I changed into my nightclothes, put out the lamp and was about to turn in when the phone rang.

'Señor Shonku?'

'Yes—'

'I'm calling from the reception. Sorry to trouble you at this hour, sir, but there's a gentleman here who is most anxious to see you.'

I said I was too tired to see anybody, and that it would be better if the gentleman could make an appointment over the phone next morning. I was sure it was a reporter. I had already been interviewed by four of them. Some of the questions they asked, tried the patience of even a placid person like me. For instance, one of them asked if crows too, like cows, were held sacred in India!

The receptionist spoke to the caller and came back to me.

'Señor Shonku, the gentleman says he wants only five minutes of your time. He has another engagement tomorrow morning.'

'This person—is he a reporter?' I asked.

'No sir. He is the famous Chilean magician Argus.'

When I heard the name, I was left with no choice but to ask him to come up. I turned on the bedside lamp. Three minutes later the buzzer sounded.

The man who confronted me when I opened the door, had seemed like a six-footer on stage; now he looked a good six inches taller. In fact, I had never seen anyone so tall before. Even when he bowed he remained a foot taller than me.

I asked him in. He had discarded his stage costume and was now dressed in an ordinary suit, but this one too was black. When he entered, I saw the evening edition of the *Correro* sticking out of his pocket. We took our seats after I had congratulated him on his performance. 'As far as I can recall,' I said, 'there was a gifted person in Greek mythology who had eyes all over his body and who was called Argus. An apt name for a magician, I think.'

Argus smiled, 'Then I'm sure you also remember that this person had some connection with birds.'

I nodded, 'The Greek goddess Hera had plucked out Argus's eyes and planted them on the peacock's tail—which is supposed to account for the circular markings on the tail. But what I'm curious about are your eyes. What is the power of your glasses?'

'Minus twenty,' he replied. 'But that doesn't bother me. None of my birds are short-sighted.'

Argus laughed loudly at his own joke, then suddenly froze open-mouthed. His eyes had strayed to the plastic cage kept on a shelf in a corner of the room. Corvus was asleep when I came in, but was now wide-awake and staring fixedly at the magician.

Argus, his mouth still open, left his chair and tiptoed towards the cage. He stared at the crow for a full minute. Then he said, 'Ever since I read about him in the evening papers, I've been anxious to meet you. I haven't had the privilege of hearing you speak. I'm not an ornithologist, you know, but I too train birds.'

The magician looked worried as he returned to his seat. 'I can well appreciate how tired you must be,' he said, 'but if you could just let your bird out of the cage . . . just one sample of his intelligence . . .'

I said, 'It's not just I who is tired; so is Corvus. I shall open the cage door for you, but the rest is up to the bird. I can't force him to do anything against his wish.'

'All right, fair enough.'

I opened the cage door. Corvus came out, flapped up to the bedside table, and with an unerring peck of his beak, switched off the lamp.

The room was plunged into darkness. Intermittent flashes of pale green light from the neon sign of the Hotel Metropole across the street glared through the open window. I sat silent. Corvus flew back to his cage and pulled the door shut with his beak.

The green light played rhythmically across Argus's face making his snake-like eyes look even more reptilian through the thick lenses of his gold-rimmed spectacles. I could see that he was struck dumb with amazement, and that he could read the meaning behind Corvus's action. Corvus wanted to rest. He didn't want light in the room. He wanted darkness; he wanted to sleep.

From under his thin moustache a soft whisper escaped his lips—'Magnifico.' He had brought his hands below his chin with his palms pressed together in a gesture of frozen applause.

Now I noticed his nails. They were unusually long and shiny. He had used nail polish—silver nail polish—the kind that would under glaring stage lights, heighten the play of his fingers. The green light was now reflected again and again on those silver nails.

'I want that crow!'

Argus spoke in English in a hoarse whisper. All this time he had been speaking in Spanish. Although, as I write this down, I realize that it probably sounds like unashamed greed, but in fact Argus was pleading with me.

'I want that crow!' Argus repeated.

I regarded him in silence. There was no need to say anything just now. I waited instead to hear what else he had to say.

Argus had been looking out of the window. Now he turned to me. I was fascinated by the alternation of darkness and light on his face. Now he was there, now he wasn't. Like magic again.

Argus moved his fingers and pointed them at himself.

'Look at me, Professor. I am Argus. I am the world's greatest magician. In every city of North and South America, anyone who knows about magic knows me. Men, women and children—they all know me. Next month I go on a world tour. Rome, Madrid, Paris, London, Athens, Stockholm, Tokyo . . . Every city will acclaim my genius. But do you know what can make my wonderful magic a thousand times more wonderful? It is that crow—that Indian crow. I want that bird, Professor, I want that bird! I do . . .'

As Argus spoke, he waved his hands before my eyes like snakes swaying to a charmer's flute, his silver nails catching the green light from the neon flashing on and off. I couldn't help being amused. If it had been anyone else in my place, Argus would have accomplished his object and got his hands on the bird. I now had to tell Argus that his plan wouldn't work with me.

I said: 'Mr Argus, you're wasting your time. It is useless to try to hypnotize me. I cannot accede to your request. Corvus is not only my pupil, he is like a son to me, and a friend—a product of my tireless effort and experiment.'

'Professor!' Argus's voice was much sharper now, but he softened it the very next moment and said, 'Professor, do you realize that I am a millionaire? Do you know that I own a fifty-room mansion in the eastern end of this city? That I have twenty-six servants and four Cadillacs? Nothing is too expensive for me, Professor. For that bird I am willing to pay you 10,000 escudos right now.'

Ten thousand escudos meant about Rs 15,000. Argus did not know that just as expenses meant nothing to him, money itself meant nothing to me. I told him so. Argus made one last attempt.

'You're an Indian. Don't you believe in mystic connections? Argus—Corvus . . . how well the two names go together! Don't you realize that the crow was fated to belong to me?'

I couldn't bear with him any more. I stood up and said, 'Mr Argus, you can keep your cars, houses, wealth and fame to yourself. Corvus is staying with me. His training is not over yet, I still have work left to do. I am extremely tired today. You had asked for five minutes of my time, and I have given you twenty. I can't give you any more. I want to sleep now and so does my bird. Therefore, good-night.'

I must say I felt faint stirrings of pity at the abject look on his face; but I didn't let them surface. Argus bowed once again in continental style and, muttering good-night in Spanish, left the room.

I closed the door and went to the cage to find Corvus still awake. Looking at me, he said 'who' in a tone which clearly suggested a question.

'A mad magician,' I told him, 'with more money than is good for him. He wanted to buy you off, but I turned him down. So you may sleep in peace.'

16 November

I wanted to record the events of yesterday last night itself, but it took me the better part of the night to get over the shock.

The way in which the day began held no hint of impending danger. In the morning there was a session of the conference, in which the only notable event was the stupendously boring extempore speech by the Japanese ornithologist Morimoto. After speaking for an hour or so, Morimoto suddenly lost the thread of his argument and started groping for words. It was at this point that Corvus, whom I had taken with me, decided to start an applause by rapping with his beak on the arm of my chair. This caused the entire audience to burst out laughing, thus putting me in an acutely embarrassing position.

In the afternoon there was lunch in the hotel with some delegates. Before going there, I went to my room, number 71, put Corvus into the cage, gave him some food and said, 'You stay here. I'm going down to eat.'

The obedient Corvus didn't demur.

By the time I finished lunch and came up, it was 2.30 p.m. As I inserted the key into the lock, a cold fear gripped me. The door was already open. I burst into the room and found my worst fears confirmed: Corvus and his cage were gone.

I was back in the corridor in a flash. Two suites down was the room-boys' enclosure. I rushed in there and found the two of them standing mutely with glazed looks in their eyes. It was clear that they had both been hypnotized.

I now ran to 107—Grenfell's room. I told him everything, and we went down to the reception together. 'No one had asked us for your room keys, sir,' said the clerk. 'The room-boys have the duplicate keys. They might have given them to someone.'

The room-boys didn't have to give the keys to anyone. Argus had cast his spell over them and helped himself to the keys.

In the end we got the real story from the concierge. He said Argus had arrived half an hour earlier in a silver Cadillac and gone into the hotel. Ten minutes later he had come out carrying a cellophane bag, got into his car and driven off.

A silver Cadillac. But where had Argus gone from here? Home? Or somewhere else?

We were now obliged to turn to the concierge for help. He said, 'I can find out for you in a minute where Argus lives; but how will that help? He is hardly likely to have gone home. He must have gone into hiding somewhere with your crow. But if he wants to leave the city, there's only one road leading out. I can fix up a good car and driver, and police personnel to go with you. But time is short. You must be out in half an hour and take the highway. If you're lucky, you may still find him.'

We were off by 3.15 p.m. Before leaving I made a phone call from the hotel and found out that Argus had not returned home. We went in a police car with two armed policemen. One of them, a young fellow named Carreras, turned out to be quite well-informed about Argus. He said Argus had several hide-outs in and around Santiago; that he had at one time hobnobbed with gypsies, and that he had been giving magic shows from the age of nineteen. About four years ago he had decided to include birds in his repertory, and this had given his popularity a great boost.

I asked Carreras if Argus was really a millionaire.

'So it would seem,' Carreras replied. 'But the man's a tightwad, and trusts nobody. That's why he has few friends left.'

As we left the city and hit the highway, we ran into a small problem. The highway branched into two—one led north to Los Andes, and the other west to the port of Valparaiso. There was a petrol station near the mouth of the fork. We asked one of the attendants there and he said, 'A silver Cadillac? Señor Argus's Cadillac? Sure, I saw it take the road to Valparaiso a little while ago.'

We shot off in pursuit. I knew Corvus would not come to any harm, as Argus needed him badly. But Corvus's behaviour last night had clearly indicated that he hadn't liked the magician at all. So it pained me to think how unhappy he must be in the clutches of his captor.

We came across two more petrol stations on the way, and both confirmed that they had seen Argus's Cadillac pass that way earlier.

I am an optimist. I have emerged unscathed from many a tight corner in the past. To this day none of my ventures has ever been a failure. But Grenfell, sitting by my side, kept shaking his head and saying, 'Don't forget, Shonku, that you're up against a fiendishly clever man. Now that he's got his hands on Corvus, it's not going to be easy for you to get your bird back.'

'And Señor Argus may be armed,' added Carreras. 'I've known him use real revolvers in his acts.'

The highway sloped downwards. From Santiago's elevation of 1600 feet, we were now down to 1000. Behind us, the mountain range was becoming progressively hazier. We had already done forty miles; another forty and we would be in Valparaiso. Grenfell's glum countenance was already beginning to make a dent in my armour of optimism. If we did not find Argus on the highway, we would have to look for him in the city, and it would then be a hundred times more difficult to track him down.

The road now rose sharply. Nothing could be seen beyond the hump. We sped along, topped the rise, and saw that the road ahead dipped gently down as far as the eye could see. A few trees dotted its sides; a village could be made out in the distance; buffaloes grazed in a field. Not a human being in sight anywhere. But what was that up ahead? It was still quite far away, whatever it was. At least a quarter of a mile.

Not more than 400 yards away now. A car, gleaming in the sunlight, parked at an angle by the roadside.

We drew nearer.

A Cadillac! A silver Cadillac!

Our Mercedes drew up alongside. Now we could see what had happened: the car had swerved and dashed against a tree. Its front was all smashed up.

'It is Señor Argus's car,' said Carreras. 'There is only one other silver Cadillac in Santiago. It belongs to the banker, Señor Galdames. I can recognize this one by its number.'

The car was there; but where was Argus?

What was that next to the driver's seat?

I poked my head through the window. It was Corvus's cage. Its key was in my pocket. I hadn't locked it that afternoon—merely put the door to. Corvus had obviously come out of the cage by himself. But after that?

Suddenly we heard someone scream in the distance. Carreras and the other policeman raised their weapons, but our driver turned out to be quite a coward. He dropped on his knees and started to pray. Grenfell's face had fallen too. 'Magicians as a tribe make me most uncomfortable,' he groaned. I said, 'I think you'd better stay in the car.'

The screams came closer. They seemed to be coming from behind some bushes, a little way ahead to the left of the road. It took me some time to recognize the voice, because last night it had been dropped to a hoarse whisper. It was the voice of Argus. He was pouring out a string of abuse in Spanish. I clearly heard 'devil' in Spanish a couple of times along with the name of my bird.

'Where is that devil of a bird? Corvus! Corvus! Damn

that bird to hell! Damn him!'

Suddenly Argus stopped, for he had seen us. We could see him too. He stood with a revolver in each hand, near some bushes about thirty yards away.

Carreras shouted, 'Lower your weapons, Señor Argus, or—'

With an ear-splitting sound a bullet came crashing into the door of our Mercedes. This was followed by three more shots, the bullets whizzing over our heads. Carreras now raised his voice threateningly. 'Señor Argus, we are fully armed. We are the police. If you don't drop your guns, we'll be forced to hurt you.'

'Hurt me?' moaned Argus in a hoarse voice. 'You are the police? I can't see anything!'

Argus was now within ten yards of us. Now I realized his plight. He had lost his spectacles, and that was why he was shooting at random.

Argus now threw down his weapons and came stumbling forward. The policemen advanced towards him. I knew that none of Argus's tricks would work in this crisis. He was in a pitiful state. Carreras retrieved the revolvers from the ground, while Argus kept groaning, 'That bird is gone—that Indian crow! That devil of a bird! But how damnably clever!'

Grenfell had been trying to say something for some time. Now at last I could make out what he was saying.

'Shonku, that bird is here.'

What did he mean? I couldn't see Corvus anywhere.

Grenfell pointed to the top of a bare acacia tree across the road.

I looked up, and sure enough, there he was: my friend, my pupil, my dear old Corvus, perched on the topmost branch of the tree and looking down at us calmly.

I beckoned, and he swooped gracefully down like a free-floating kite and alighted on the roof of the Mercedes. Then, carefully, as if he was fully aware of its worth, he placed before us the object he had been carrying in his beak: Argus's high-powered, gold-rimmed spectacles.

Translated by Satyajit Ray

ACKNOWLEDGEMENTS

'The Diary of a Space Traveller' first appeared in *Sandesh*, 1961; 'Professor Shonku and the Bones' first appeared in *Sandesh*, 1963; 'Professor Shonku and the Macaw' first appeared in *Sandesh*, 1964; 'Professor Shonku and the Mysterious Sphere' first appeared in *Sandesh*, 1965; 'Professor Shonku and Chee-ching' first appeared in *Sandesh*, 1965; 'Professor Shonku and the Little Boy' first appeared in *Sandesh*, 1967; 'Professor Shonku and the Spook' first appeared in *Ashchorjo*, 1966; 'Professor Shonku and Robu' first appeared in *Sandesh*, 1968; 'Professor Shonku and the Egyptian Terror' first appeared in *Sandesh*, 1963; 'Professor Shonku and the Curious Statuettes' first appeared in *Sandesh*, 1965; 'Professor Shonku and the Box from Baghdad' first appeared in *Sandesh*, 1970; 'Corvus' first appeared in *Anandamela*, 1972.

Read more in Puffin

The Unicorn Expedition

Satyajit Ray

Illustrated by Agantuk

Professor Shonku cannot dismiss without proof the possibility that unicorns do exist somewhere on earth. In fact, Charles Willard, a fellow scientist, claimed to have actually seen them in Tibet, but, unfortunately, died shortly afterwards. So, when Shonku learns that another expedition is starting off for Tibet, he jumps at the opportunity to trace Willard's route and find the unicorns.

Tibet is just one of the exotic places Professor Shonku's exploits take him in this volume of stories. In the Sahara Desert he comes face to face with a massive pyramid-like structure no one knew of earlier, he travels underwater in a submarine with two Japanese scientists to investigate the sudden appearance of deadly red fish that have taken to eating humans, in the caves of Bolivia he meets a primitive man who has been painting his dwelling with animal figures and strange mathematical formulae, and on a peculiar island which has appeared out of nowhere in the Pacific Ocean horrific plants suck out all his learning from his brain.

Professor Shonku is at the height of his ingenuity and daring in this collection, and thrills and surprises await us around every bend as we follow him on his astonishing adventures.

Translated from the Bengali by Satyajit Ray and Gopa Majumdar.

A PUFFIN ORIGINAL
Fiction
India Rs 250

Read more in Puffin

Abol Tabol: The Nonsense World of Sukumar Ray

Sukumar Ray

Illustrated by the author

Masterpieces from the king of nonsense

The Bengali language has never been quite so much a living, breathing creature of whimsy as in Sukumar Ray's hands, and his creations – wild and wicked, dreamy and delirious – have thrilled children and adults alike. This selection offers you the best of his world – pun-riddled, fun-fiddled poetry from *Abol Tabol* and *Khai-Khai*, stories of schoolboy pranks (*Pagla Dashu*) and madcap explorers (*Heshoram Hushiyarer Diary*), and the unforgettable harum-scarum classic *Haw-Jaw-Baw-Raw-Law*, presented here for the first time in its entirety. All the stories and poems are accompanied by Sukumar Ray's inimitable illustrations.

Sampurna Chattarji's lively new translation captures the magical nonsense groove of the Bengali original through a freewheeling play of sound and sense. This is a book that is sure to captivate Sukumar Ray fans and win him a whole new generation of admirers.

Translated from the Bengali by Sampurna Chattarji

A PUFFIN ORIGINAL
Fiction
India Rs 199

Read more in Penguin

Abel [illegible]: The Notorious [illegible]

[illegible]

[illegible]

[illegible]

[illegible]

[illegible]

[illegible]

Read more in Puffin

Goopy Gyne Bagha Byne: The Magical World of Upendrakishore Roy Choudhury

Upendrakishore Roy Choudhury

Illustrated by Dipankar Bhattacharya

Wondrous encounters with magical characters

Goopy and Bagha are really bad musicians who are cast out of their homes because their music drives their families and neighbours crazy. In the forest, they meet the king of ghosts, and pleased with their music, he grants them boons which change their lives.

Meet the little tuntuni bird, the clever fox, Majantali Sarkar the cat, the clever grandmother, and many other fascinating creatures who fill the pages of this book.

Upendrakishore Roy Choudhury is one of the best-known Bengali writers for children, and Swagata Deb's vibrant translation brings his unique magic to a wider audience.

Translated from the Bengali by Swagata Deb

A PUFFIN ORIGINAL
Fiction
India Rs 199

Read more in Puffin

The Prince and Other Modern Fables

Rabindranath Tagore

Illustrated by Rosy Rodrigues

Fairy tales with a difference

India's greatest poet of modern times, Nobel Prize-winning author Rabindranath Tagore was a philosopher, a visionary and a storyteller par excellence. His short, lyrical prose fables, set in a generic fairyland or in everyday locales, are philosophical excursions across magical landscapes that speak to the imaginative child in every reader.

The pages of **The Prince and Other Modern Fables** are full of insightful little stories that reveal the simple truth about life. There is the story of a little boy who has lost his mother, of a tribal girl who is mistaken for a fairy, of a jester who watches a king fight his battles from the sidelines, of a young man who tries to come to terms with his first heartache, and of a modern-day prince who is trying to eke out a living in the unforgiving city. Asking questions that we usually don't stop to ask ourselves, and often coming up with answers that are surprising in their simplicity, every story sparkles with insights on the human condition, and remain etched in the mind long afterwards.

Now available in a lucid and vibrant translation, this classic collection is sure to enchant modern readers who might never have encountered it before.

Translated from the Bengali by Sreejata Guha

A PUFFIN ORIGINAL
Fiction
India Rs 150

PENGUIN ONLINE

News, reviews and previews of forthcoming books

visit our author lounge

•

read about your favourite authors

•

investigate over 12000 titles

•

subscribe to our online newsletter

•

enter contests and quizzes and win prizes

•

email us with your comments and reviews

•

have fun at our children's corner

•

receive regular email updates

•

keep track of events and happenings

www.penguinbooksindia.com